The Reverse of the Curse Series, Book 2

Vampires 200

R. Stone

This is a work of fiction. Names, characters, places, and incidents are products of the author's imagination or are used fictitiously and are not to be construed as real. Any resemblance to actual events, locales, organizations, or persons, living or dead, is entirely coincidental.

This book whether in hard copy or e-book is licensed for your personal enjoyment only. It may not be re-sold or given away to other people. If you would like to share this book with another person, please purchase an additional copy for each recipient.

The Reverse of the Curse Series ° Copyright 2013
Vampires 200
R. Stone

Cover Artist: Tatiana Vila
Formatted by: Jesse Gordon
Publisher: Shelly Stone
Editor: Shelly Stone

ISBN: 10-0615795501
ISBN: 13-978-0615795508

Pre-requisite to this book is "Vampires 101."
Vampires 201, out in April of 2014.

Dedicated to: My children Jeremy and Nicole

1

KICK BUTT HUMAN

I stood in our living room and looked at my brother. "The mall, you want me to go to the mall with her, why?" I had never seen Alexander act like this over a woman before, especially a human one.

"Antoinette, you promised me that you would try to get to know her."

"No Alexander, I promised you that I wouldn't bite her head off."

"And then, you promised me that you would go to the mall with her. She will be here in about an hour and she wants to get a pair of boots at the mall, she is really excited about spending some time with you!"

"Alright, Alexander if you will excuse me then I will just go upstairs and get dressed for the occasion." "I would force myself to enjoy it", I thought.

"Thanks, sis, I won't forget this. I am going upstairs to my office I need to send that email to Principle Hines with our course outline for "Vampires 200" for next semester."

* * *

I sat at my desk in my medical clinic on the third floor of our three-story Victorian-style home trying to work while Antoinette got dressed, but I couldn't concentrate. I was thinking about Ariel, it had only been two weeks since she had confronted me in the teacher's lounge at school about being a vampire. My initial attempt to deny it failed and she saw through the façade and persisted to the point that I took her into my confidence. I felt overwhelmed, both as a doctor and a vampire, both were my entire life and world and I knew the risk of letting Ariel into it. My thoughts were interrupted when my cell phone rang I picked it up and hit the talk button. "Yes hello."

"Hello, Alexander it is Principle Hines."

"Hello Sir."

"I hope I am not disturbing you Alexander, but I just wanted to remind you to send me that e-mail with your course outline for next semester."

"Yes Sir, I am sitting at my desk now and I will send it in just a moment."

6

"Thanks and Alexander I've got some good news for you, I got your classes approved for college credit. It was approved because of your and Antoinette's teaching credentials, so now your students will earn one college credit when they take your classes."

"Oh, thank you Sir, that is good news."

"You are welcome, goodbye Alexander."

"Goodbye Sir." I hung up the phone and hit the send button in my email. My thoughts drifted back to Ariel and when we had first met, I was instantly attracted to her and an unbreakable bond had formed between us. I only wished my conversation last night with Antoinette had gone better, she took the news badly and I had to make her promise not to bite Ariel's head off.

* * *

I had already gotten dressed and lay on my bed in my room waiting for Ariel to arrive. I was still infuriated with Alexander since he had told me that he was dating Ariel. "What is it that he saw in her?" I wondered. She is a five-foot, two-inch tall clumsy human with red hair and green-eyes. He had never had a human girlfriend before. "What was it about her that made him trust her with our secret? Why would he jeopardize all of this for her?" We had spent hundreds of years researching and preparing for this moment and we were the only two doctors in the entire world that had the knowledge of how to change a vampire back to a human. "Didn't he get how serious this was?" These thoughts kept running through my mind. I rolled over in my bed and sighed, but it didn't help, he just expected me to accept his decision and I had no choice but to tolerate her presence both at Lincoln High where we taught our classes and then here in our home, whenever she visited! "I should be happy for him he hasn't had a girlfriend in a long time", I thought, but no matter how I tried to remind myself of that, it didn't work. "What is it about her that I don't like?" I asked myself. She is nice enough, I thought. Maybe that was it! Maybe she is too nice - the catholic school virgin nice. Alexander had told me that she only had one other boyfriend in her entire life and wouldn't it just figure - she had to fall in love with my brother – the vampire. I had this nagging feeling in the pit of my stomach about Ariel ever since the first time I'd met her.

I heard the doorbell ring and knew that it was Ariel arriving for her visit with Alexander and our trip to the mall. I sat up in my bed and instantly recalled my promise to Alexander, to make an effort to get to know her and then the realization hit that it was at times like this – that the responsibility of being a sister far out weighed the benefits!

I heard Alexander call out to me. "Antoinette, we have company, come on down." I stood from my bed and walked out of my room. I wouldn't enjoy my walk down the staircase today or slide down the banister at the last set of stairs and land in the foyer, like I usually did instead I walked slowly down the staircase, one step at a time. When I reached the bottom of the stairs I saw Alexander standing with Ariel in the foyer.

Ariel looked at me and smiled. "Hello Antoinette, how are you?"

I looked at her and returned the smile. She looked as clumsy as ever, her curly frizzed-out red hair hung loosely around her face, and fell just past her shoulder's, she almost looked to petite to have so much hair. Her pale white skin and big round green eyes and thick lashes reminded me of one of those baby dolls, where the eyes almost looked too big for the face and she only weighed about a hundred pounds. I just didn't see what my brother saw in this weak fragile human. "Hello Ariel" I said and then walked past the both of them and into the living room. I didn't want to go to the mall with her, but I had promised, it was part of the "Get to know Ariel campaign!" I plopped down in one of the big oversized easy chairs that faced the couch. I imagine that my face looked rather un-inviting but I didn't care, I sat here just like I promised. I watched Alexander and Ariel walk into the living room and sit down side by side on the couch.

Ariel turned to Alexander. "Oh you won't believe what happened today in my afternoon Greek Mythology class?"

I looked at them sitting on the couch and Ariel looked like a small teenager sitting next to an adult. Alexander was just over six foot tall and had brown eyes and brown hair like me. I watched my brother's eyes light up when he spoke to her. "What happened?"

"Well, I've got this group of kids in my class, three guys and three girls, actually they are more like a gang and they got pretty hard to handle today."

I looked at my brother and could tell that he felt extraordinarily protective of Ariel.

Alexander slid closer to her. "Are you ok? Tell me what happened."

Ariel smiled. "Oh, I am fine now, but these guys were very disruptive. They talked during class, swore a couple of times, and then threw their books at each other.

When I tried to get them to quiet down, one of the guys swore at me."

I watched the hairs stand up on the back of Alexander's neck, that meant he was angry.

"You should have come to my classroom and got me Ariel I could have helped you with them."

Ariel smiled. "Oh, I couldn't involve you like that, I left the classroom and went and got Principle Hines and he took care of it. He told them one more instance like that and they would be suspended."

"That's good Ariel." I watched while Alexander turned his head to me. "Isn't that good Antoinette?"

I could tell that he was trying to involve me in the conversation. I leaned forward in my chair. "Yes, that is good they deserve to be suspended if they act like that again." I silently thought about what I might do if I had some teenagers in my class like that and then I smiled. I pictured myself throwing a book at them with such speed that no one would even see me do it, but I realized that as the teacher I shouldn't do something like that. I looked at Ariel. "Well, Ariel we really should get going if we are going to shop at the mall it's already six-thirty and the mall closes at nine, we will have a few hours there at best." I just wanted to get there and get this over with as quickly as possible. Alexander and Ariel stood up and I followed them to the door. I watched while Alexander kissed Ariel goodbye, "I'll see you tomorrow at school."

Ariel walked out the door and to her car, I looked at her tiny little dark blue beetle sitting in our driveway. "Oh, I can't wait", I thought.

Alexander and I stood in the doorway, he turned to me, "And you sister be nice to her and get to know her, like you promised me."

"Yes, I promised, but doesn't it worry you that she knows about us? Why is it that you trust her so much, what if she tells someone? It could jeopardize all of our hard work."

"Antoinette I didn't tell her, she guessed and I could not lie to her, she's smart, smarter than most humans and you've read her thoughts yourself, you know she won't say anything, so what is it that is really bothering you about her?"

"She's human, that's enough isn't it? She is frail and weak. I am curious, what is it that she could possibly offer you? She is more like a liability than an asset." I watched while he put his head down. I hadn't meant for it to come out quite like that and I could tell that I'd hurt his feelings.

"I don't see her like that, yes she is human and weaker than us, but she is also full of life and is a really great person and I expect you to take care of her while your out."

I smirked at him. "Of course I will."

"It's not funny, Antoinette you have a knack for running into trouble, no dark alleys or walks downtown or parking garages, she is important to me."

"Ok, Alexander, I'll avoid trouble and keep her safe while we shop, I promise."

I left Alexander standing in the doorway and walked outside and got into the beetle. Ariel looked over at me with those big green baby-doll eyes. "Please buckle up Antoinette, it's the law."

I gritted my teeth and smiled as I drew the seat belt out and around my body and secured it. "This car is so little, how can you stand it?"

"Oh, I love it, it's so cute!"

"Great, this is going to be a blast", I thought.

Ariel pulled up to the mall and we found the parking lot completely full. "Oh, it looks like we will have to park in the underground garage."

"Terrific, I had promised Alexander no alleys or parking garages", I thought. "Ariel, let's circle round one more time, maybe we will find a spot."

"No, it's alright, the garage will do", Ariel said and then drove into the underground parking garage and found a vacant spot and parked. We got out of the roller skate, "That's what I would call it from now on", I told myself. We entered the mall and I paused just inside the doorway, "Ariel, is there anywhere in particular that you want to go to?"

"No, nowhere specific but I would like to look for a pair of black high-heeled boots while we walk around."

"Great, then if you don't mind I want to check out Neiman Marcus, it's my favorite store." I took the lead and Ariel trailed alongside me.

"Oh, they have some really great stuff, but I can't afford to shop there, but I'll look while you shop."

We walked into Neiman Marcus. Ariel's comment stuck with me, I shopped here all the time but I had never really thought about other's who couldn't afford to. We walked through Neiman Marcus and I collected an armful of blouses.

"Wow, Antoinette, you have so many blouses, can I help you carry some of them?"

"No, thanks I am fine, I just love clothes and I consider myself an avid collector. I probably have about a hundred blouses in my closet."

Ariel – looked over at me. "Wow, those are really pretty but you haven't looked at one price tag, don't you care how much they cost?"

I turned my head toward Ariel. "No, I don't care I spend a lot of my pay checks on clothes and shoes, I also love fur." I smiled, "I guess this is all part of getting to know her, Alexander you owe me big time!" I thought.

"That's nice, Antoinette. I have been saving my money for a down payment on a town house, so that I can get out of my apartment by next summer."

I looked over at Ariel. "Poor simple-minded, human", I thought. "That's nice Ariel." We walked toward the register and then I paid for my stuff and we left Neiman Marcus. "Ariel, why don't I just follow you for a while?"

"Okay", she said and took the lead. After a few minutes I followed Ariel into a small shoe store and waited while she looked for a pair of boots. "Cool, look at these boots, this is just what I have been looking for", she said and then took the black leather high-heeled boots off the shelf. "Size-five, just my size I am going to get these."

I looked over at Ariel. "Size-five, I wear a size-eight I couldn't get my toes into those things." Ariel tried the boots on and then paid for them and we left. We walked around the mall for about another hour and then we heard the announcement. "The mall will be closing in five minutes will all patrons please make their way toward the exits."

"Well, this was fun Ariel I guess we'd better get going?" We walked side by side out the door of the mall and into the parking garage it was almost empty and there were only two cars left on the level where we had parked. I watched while Ariel walked ahead of me swinging her shopping bag back and forth like a teenager and then all of a sudden four guys stepped out from behind one of the big cement columns that separated the parking rows. By their dress, hair and tattoos it was obvious that they belonged to one of the local gangs in Portland. Ariel stopped walking and I quickly moved to her side. I knew that to the average woman they looked scary, but they didn't frighten me. All of a sudden my promise to Alexander flashed in my mind, "No alleys or parking garages", and here I stood with Ariel at my side in an underground parking garage facing a gang of four guys who looked like they meant to do us harm. I knew that if anything happened to her Alexander probably wouldn't forgive me.

"Hey, girls, where are you going so fast? Why don't you hang out with us for a while?" one of the guys said and then he took a step toward us.

I stepped closer to Ariel and knew that it would be up to me to defend the both of us. I had no intention of killing them, especially in front of her, but a good butt-kicking wouldn't hurt them.

"Don't move Ariel, just stand perfectly still", I told her.

Another one of the guys moved toward us. "Hey come on over and visit with us?"

Before I had a chance to react I saw Ariel drop her bag and lunge toward the guy closest to us and deliver some kind of karate chop to his throat. He doubled over and gasped for air.

I watched the next guy that stood closest to us move toward her, "Hey, shrimp", he said and attempted to grab her by the arm, but she dodged his attack and grabbed his arm and twisted it behind his back, I heard a quick snap and knew that she had broke his arm. "My arm, my arm is broke", he cried and stumbled back-wards.

"Hey girl, over here?" the third member of the gang said and ran toward her. Ariel simply stepped back and did a round house with her leg and the left side of her foot connected with his jaw. "Dam, my jaw is broke."

I dropped my bags and just stood there watching in disbelief, everything was happening so fast, human fast.

The fourth guy reached out and grabbed her by her hair. She dropped down into a squatting position in front of him while he still held her hair in his hand and she punched him below the belt. He let go of her hair and doubled over. One by one I watched them run off.

Ariel stood up and was breathing hard. "Whew, it's been a while since I had to use that", she said and then picked up her bags.

"Are you alright, Antoinette?"

I just stood there with my mouth wide open. This little five-foot two-inch woman just kicked the butts of four guys. "You're a black-belt?"

"A triple black belt, my dad was an instructor."

"Wow Ariel, that was pretty amazing, for a human I mean."

We walked over to the little beetle and got in. "Buckle up it's the law", Ariel said. I buckled my seat belt and she sped off.

"Ariel, just so you know, I was prepared to defend both of us?"

"I know Antoinette, you could have killed those guys, but I can take care of myself."

I looked over at her while she drove and wondered how much she knew about Alexander and I. "Ariel, how much has Alexander told you about us?"

"Not a lot. He told me that he doesn't kill and feeds from the blood he gets at the two blood banks where you both do volunteer work."

"What did he tell you about me?" I don't know why I'd asked her but I wondered if Alexander had told her about how I occasionally feed on a murderer or two and then and I wondered how she felt about that?

"Well, Alexander told me that you have different views about feeding and that you hunt killers."

"Yes, that is correct."

"Those, guys at the mall are they the kind of guys that you would go after?"

"No, not them, I would have liked to kick their butts though. Usually I read someone's thoughts first to see what kind of person they are and if they intend to murder, then they are fair game."

"Oh."

Ariel pulled the car up in front of my house and I got out. "Thanks Ariel, I'll see you tomorrow at school", I told her and walked into the house.

As soon as I had entered the house, I saw Alexander standing in the foyer with that look on his face. I recognized the look instantly it was his "What did I tell you look" and then I realized that he knew what had happened at the mall. "Here it comes", I thought.

"One thing, Antoinette – I asked you for just one thing, no alleys or parking garages and you couldn't even do that."

I looked at him. "Did you follow us?" I asked him but by the look on his face I already knew that he had.

"I am sorry I was worried about her, that's been happening a lot lately, I've been having these really uneasy feelings about her and I don't know why."

"So then you saw what happened, you saw her kick those guys butts." I watched while Alexander ran his hand through his hair. "Yes I did and I was very surprised."

I smiled. "Didn't you know that she was a triple black belt?"

"No, Antoinette I didn't, but that's not the point. That stuff only works on humans, you know that. If those guys had been vampires the two of you would have been out numbered and dead."

"I can handle myself."

"Not against four vampires, you can't, nor could she, so don't be too mad at me for following the two of you – we are new to this area and we don't know how many other vampires are around. I wasn't just worried about her I have been worried about you too ever since you told me about that night you went to the mall in Beaverton, when that guy tried to attack you."

"Yes, but that guy was a human."

"I understand Antoinette, but we are not in England anymore, we are in a huge metropolitan city and there are a lot of vampires here and vampire gangs out on the streets too – I really would prefer knowing where you are at all times. If anything happens to you mom, dad and nana Victoria would never forgive me."

"Fine, Alexander…I am going to go upstairs and try on my shirts from Neiman Marcus, we've got a big day tomorrow, first day of a new semester."

2

WELCOME TO VAMPIRES 200

I sat in the school gymnasium and watched Principle Hines walk up to the podium and flick the microphone with his finger tip before he began to speak in it. This was the morning gathering of faculty and students and I knew that Principle Hines would be talking to everyone about the recent vandalisms to school property.

He called everyone to order and began speaking. "Now that I have everyone's attention, I will begin. I am sure that you all know why you have been called here. I feel it necessary to discuss the recent vandalisms that have occurred on school grounds and inform you directly that this kind of behavior will not be tolerated and it needs to stop immediately. Even though I do not know who is responsible, it is only a matter of time before I find out. Surveillance cameras have been installed in various locations throughout the school, but I also have my own ways of finding out information and when I do, I can assure you that whoever is responsible for this will be dealt with harshly - not just here at the school but also by local law enforcement. The windows of the school kitchen were broken out last night and a couple of weeks ago some of the students lockers and one of the teachers lounges had been broken into. This will stop immediately! In the history of this school, this is the worst year ever for this type of conduct. I encourage any of you who know anything about this to report it to my office immediately, you will be provided with amnesty. If this continues I will be forced to cancel the upcoming school dance. That is all you are dismissed and may return to your classes."

I sat next to Alexander and Ariel on the wooden bleachers. After Principle Hines finished speaking we stood up and stepped down from the bleachers and then walked outside. I waited while Alexander gave Ariel a small kiss on the cheek and they said their goodbyes. "How ridiculous, it's only nine in the morning and you will see each other at lunch", I thought.

Ariel walked away and I looked over at my brother. "Please, Alexander, give me a break?"

"What do you mean?"

"It looked like you two were saying goodbye for days, not just a few hours."

"Funny Antoinette let's get to class."

"Yes, I am excited it is the first day of our new class Vampires 200." I followed Alexander to our classroom and stood behind him while he unlocked the classroom door. We stepped inside and stood near the door.

"Well Antoinette, I hope that we have more vampire students this semester than last semester."

"Yes, I do too. I am still surprised that last semester Emma was our only vampire student, but I am happy that we were able to change her and her family back to humans."

"Yes, it did bring me a lot of joy to change Emma, Charles, Eloise and Lucy back. Still, I do hope that we have more vampire students this semester."

The bell rang.

I watched the students walk in one at a time and take a seat. I saw three of my students from "Vampires 101", Mirka, Joseph, and Lauren walk in.

"Hello, Antoinette", Joseph said.

"Hello, to all of you I am glad to see you back again."

They took their seats. The rest of the students entered and took their seats.

Alexander and I stepped toward the front of the room and my eyes began scanning the classroom. I saw a group of kids sitting together in the rear of the room, they looked like an intimate little group and I knew instantly that they were all vampires, there were seven of them. I turned my head to Alexander and it was as if he had read my thoughts, we did that sometimes, being brother and sister. He looked at me and nodded his head. My ears sifted through the background noise of the class while all the students talked and I could hear the vampire group quietly conversing about Alexander and I. I heard their comments flying back and forth between them "What's up with this?" – "What are they doing here?" – "Oh, man we need to drop this class fast" – "No, this could be interesting."

I smiled. They were apparently shocked that Alexander and I were vampires. Alexander took control of the classroom.

"Hello class and welcome to Vampires 200 Anatomy and Morphology of the Vampire, part one. My name is Dr. Alexander Von-Allenberg and I would like to introduce my co-teacher and sister Dr. Antoinette Von-Allenberg. Both Antoinette and I are Professors in our fields of Science and Teaching, so you may address us in several different ways, by Professor, by Mr. or Ms. Von-Allenberg or simply by Alexander or Antoinette, we will leave that up to you individually. Class will meet daily for eight weeks and part two of this class will be offered next semester in a class called Vampires 201. I would like to go around the room for a brief moment and let each of you introduce yourselves. Let's start with this row", I said and then pointed to the first student in the first row.

"I am Dan", "Mirka", "Joseph", "Lauren", "I am Melissa" "Levi", "Hope", "I am Troy", "Karla", "Jake", "I am Amy."

I stood next to Alexander and looked at each of the vampire students one at a time before they introduced their selves and their thoughts became mine. The big blonde-haired guy with blue eyes was around seventeen and he was the leader, his thoughts bothered me, he was a hunter and a stalker and had no regard for human life, he introduced himself, "I am Luke", the brown-haired girl in the desk next to him was his mate and not much different from him, "I am Darla", she said. The two guys who sat behind Luke both had dark hair and dark eyes and also shared Luke's feeling of little regard for human life, "I am Jason" and "I am Matt." There were two females that sat behind Darla. One of the girls was petite with black hair and bright blue eyes, she reminded me of Emma and when I looked at her and read her thoughts I felt fear, "I am Mia", she said. The girl that sat next to her had brown hair and brown eyes, and I also sensed fear in her, "I am Tara." I looked at the next member of their group and he was the youngest, I guessed his age at around fourteen. He was a short thin oriental boy and when I'd read his thoughts I'd felt sorry for him, he was truly afraid, my guess was that he was the newest member of the group of vampires, "I am Dorian."

"Excellent, thank you all, I will turn the class over to my sister Antoinette."

Alexander stepped away from me and walked to his desk and sat down to work on his medical papers while I handled the class. I cleared my throat. "Ok, class, I am going to start with a recap of our "Vampires 101" course that we taught last semester. I won't spend too much time on it, probably just this morning and then from there we will move on to talking about the anatomy of the vampire. Eight weeks goes by fast and as Alexander mentioned earlier part-two of this class will be offered next semester as "Vampires 201", any questions, before we get started?"

When Luke raised his hand – I knew that he would make some unnecessary smart remark.

"Yes, Luke?"

He looked at me for a moment and I felt as though he was trying to read my thoughts, then I wondered if he had the gift like I did, but I doubted it because of the blank look on his face and concluded that he was just trying to psych me out. He finally spoke.

"Vampires don't have an anatomy, they are dead", he said and then laughed and then everyone in his group laughed. The rest of the class remained silent.

I'd sensed that the other kids in my class were afraid of Luke and his friends. I couldn't blame them, they did look pretty rough. I smiled at him. "Oh Luke, I can assure you that vampires do have an anatomy and I know everything about it. I know both a vampire's strengths and their WEAKNESSES!" I emphasized the word "Weaknesses" with my voice and it caught his attention. I believe he had caught the underlying threat in my message. He glared at me with his piercing blue eyes and when I'd read his thoughts again - I knew that I had made him angry. "Alright, if there are no more questions we will get started. Last semester we discussed some myths and legends about vampires, essentially the history of the vampire. We talked about how vampires first surfaced during the eleventh-century. I explained how the various accounts of vampires and vampire related incidents prior to the eleventh-century were probably not really vampire – related. It is mine and Alexander's theory that the vampire did not exist before the eleventh-century and that any incidents that date before the eleventh-century, like a body that was found drained of its blood can be explained by a myriad of other things, — like "The blood-letting process." This was a medical procedure where doctors used to drain the blood of their patients because they thought that any disease that the patient had would come out with the blood. Most patients treated by this procedure died from a massive loss of blood. When bodies like this were dug up by — doctors or archeologists later, analysis showed that the bodies contained little blood in the tissues. These bodies often got confused with what I call the "Real Victims" of a vampire."

I saw a hand go up. "Yes Troy?"

"What do you mean by real victims of a vampire?"

I looked at him. "Well Troy, I believe that the bodies found that date before the eleventh-century, are victims of the blood-letting process. Bodies found — in the eleventh-century and later not only had their blood drained but had other characteristics present that are related to vampires." I saw a hand go up. "Yes, Hope."

"What kind of characteristics?"

"Good, question Hope, well for instance the heads had been severed from the body or the body had been cut in half or the bodies had been buried with garlic, or mirrors or other things that are related to vampires – and vampire stories."

I saw another hand go up it was Darla, one of the vampires. "Yes, Darla?"

"So you do not believe that vampires existed before the eleventh-century?"

"Yes, Darla you are correct, I do not believe that vampires existed before the eleventh-century."

Darla looked confused. "Why, who said that they didn't?"

I looked at Darla and read her thoughts, her question had been genuine and she really was curious as to why I didn't believe that vampires existed before the eleventh-century. This pleased me I had caught the attention of my vampire students.

"Darla there is not much documented about vampires that, dates prior to the eleventh-century, but after the eleventh-century you will find a lot of information." I had hoped that my answer would suffice. I certainly couldn't tell her that I knew for certain – that vampires didn't exist prior – to the eleventh-century because Alexander had created them during the eleventh-century when his medical experiment had gone bad.

"That makes sense", Darla said.

Luke raised his hand again. "Yes, Luke?"

I watched while he laughed and tried to get hold of himself before he spoke. "So Antoinette have you ever seen a vampire?"

"Yes, Luke I have." He hadn't expected me to admit that. The entire class had their eyes on me. "I mean that I've seen corpses that have been exhumed that look like vampires, corpses that have been staked through the heart, buried with garlic or mirrors, and had elongated teeth and claw-like finger nails – things like that." My students looked shocked. "You can google this stuff on the internet and find lots of cases like this." I had killed Luke's potential for an argument and I could tell by the look on his face that he didn't like it. He glared at me. I could feel Alexander glaring back at Luke from behind me trying to relay the message to Luke to back off.

The bell rang.

I watched the students pick up their books and walk out of the classroom. Luke and his group took their time and stood by their desks for a moment. I watched while Darla handed her books to Mia, the vampire girl with the black hair and blue eyes that reminded me of Emma.

"It's your turn Mia to carry my books for a while." I watched while Mia took the books from Darla and didn't say a word. I sensed that she was afraid of Darla. I smiled and thought about what Emma might have done in that situation, she would have thrown the books in Darla's face and told her to carry her own books. I watched while Mia tried to stack Darla's books on top of her own and it wasn't working. Tara took half the books from Mia. "Here Mia, I'll take some", she said and stacked them on top of her own books.

"Thanks Tara", Mia said.

Luke began to lead his group out of the classroom. "Let's take a break and go to the cafeteria and check out the menu?" He said. They all laughed, and walked out of the classroom.

I knew what Luke had meant – vampires don't eat, he'd meant the human menu. I knew that this group would be a problem.

Alexander got up from his desk and walked over and stood beside me. "Antoinette, they are going to be a big problem."

"I know, but that's what we'd hoped for troubled vampires that we could help."

"Antoinette, I don't think Luke wants our help!"

3

TROUBLE IN THE CAFETERIA

Tara gave my shoulder a slight push from behind. "Hurry, Mia" she said while we walked through the doors of the cafeteria. I followed Luke, Matt, Jason and Darla into the cafeteria and Tara and Dorian trailed behind me. I stepped through the door and watched as Darla walked ahead of me, arm in arm with Luke. They were inseparable, Luke breathed Darla breathed. Luke was pure evil and Darla thrived on that, she was like him. Matt and Jason weren't much better than Luke, they could be pretty wicked and in fact I believe that they wished they were Luke.

Darla turned around and looked at me, "Hurry up Mia", she said.

"Coming, Darla." I watched while they walked ahead of me and thought about when Tara and I first joined their group. I remembered how happy I was when we first found them, but then we realized it was a mistake to hook up with them and now we just wanted to get away but they wouldn't let us.

"Here babe, have a seat", Luke said and held out a chair for Darla to sit down.

"Thanks sweetie."

Luke carelessly plopped down in a seat next to Darla and then pushed his chair back and raised his legs and rested them on the cafeteria table. "That's better", Luke said. Luke looked up at Matt, Jason, Dorian and Tara. "Take a seat peasants." Matt and Jason sat down on the same side of the table as Luke, and Dorian and Tara sat opposite Luke. Tara looked up at me, "Aren't you going to sit down Mia?"

I looked at Luke and Darla. "I am going to go over and look at the bulletin board, I'll be right back." I felt like such a child to have to always tell them where I went or what I did. I wished we could just run from them, but I'd seen what happened to others who tried that. I had decided to just play it cool for a while until I could plan an escape. I walked over to the bulletin board and looked at a poster about the upcoming school dance, I stood gazing at it. I wouldn't attend my Junior or Senior prom or have a normal life ever again. I saw a map of the school grounds, it showed the main building, the principles office, teacher's lounges, library, the

gym, the student library, the art room and the maintenance building. "Home sweet home" – I thought and
smiled.

Matt walked up and stood next to me. "See anything
interesting Mia?"

I knew that Matt liked me. "Not much, our house is
right there", I said and pointed to the maintenance
building and then laughed.

"That's really funny, Mia."

I pointed to a flyer about the dance. "This looks like
fun." Matt looked at the flyer. I turned back around and
looked at the table where the others sat, I saw Luke sur-
veying the cafeteria and I knew two things, either he was
looking for someone to harass or he was looking for his
next meal. Luke got up from the table and walked over
to the student who sat at his table alone eating lunch.
Luke bumped the student with his arm and the student's
lunch tray slid off the table and hit the floor.

"Whoops, sorry bout that dude", he said.

The student looked up at Luke and didn't say a word.

Everyone laughed.

Luke returned to the table and Darla stood up and
wrapped her arms around Luke's neck and kissed him.
"Good one babe."

"Yes, he had it coming."

Matt walked away from the bulletin board and returned to the table and sat down. I could hear Matt talking with Luke, "Mia said she saw a flyer about a dance, what do you think?" Their voices faded out of my head. Everyone was staring at us, everywhere we went Luke drew attention. I walked back to our table and sat down and looked around the cafeteria at the other kids and I saw a blonde haired girl staring at me from a couple of tables over. I recognized her from our vampire class her name was Melissa.

* * *

"They look like a real gang Erin?"

"Who are you talking about Melissa?"

"That group over there, they are in my vampire class. Do you know anything about them?"

Erin turned his head away from me to look at them and then turned back around. "No way Melissa, I am a jock I don't hang out with scum like that."

"True that, they look like trouble", Levi said.

I turned to Levi. "What do you know about them?"

"Not much Melissa, I heard that they got kicked out of another high school in Portland." I looked over at them again. "That doesn't surprise me, they look like gothic freaks they remind me of that girl from last semester from my English class....what was her name?"

Levi looked at me. "Melissa you know what her name was, it was Emma, you should remember it, she kicked your butt."

I looked at Levi and raised my eyebrows. "She didn't kick my butt she just got a lucky push when I wasn't looking." Some other kids at a nearby table caught my eye. "Hey, Levi isn't that the Russian girl sitting over there, you know the one that's in our class, Mirka or Marka, or something like that."

"Sitting where Melissa?"

"Over there, at that table?" I said and tilted my head sideways trying to make an effort to point at her without it being noticeable.

Levi turned his head slightly. "I think so, why?"

"No reason, just wondering."

"If you minded your own business Melissa – you wouldn't get yourself into so much trouble", Levi said.

"You got that right", Erin said.

"Shut up Erin, you're my boyfriend you are supposed to be on my side."

Erin laughed. "See you later Melissa, come on Levi, we need to get going we are going to be late for football practice."

* * *

"Mirka, that blonde chick is staring at you?"

"Where at Joseph"

"Over there at that table, do you know her?"

I turned my head to look. "I don't think so, but she looks familiar."

Lauren turned her head toward me. "Mirka, she's in our class."

I looked at Lauren. "Which class?"

"Our vampire class her name is Melissa."

"That's right. Why is she staring at me like that?"

"Just ignore it baby?" Joseph said.

I turned my head to Joseph, "Don't call me baby, you know I hate it."

"I know Mirka, that's why I do it. You are my best friend and if you can't annoy your best friend, who then?"

Lauren turned in her chair. "Hey Mirka, if you really want to look at something, check them out over there, they are in our class too."

I looked over my shoulder. "Oh, that's Luke, Darla and their friends, they started at Lincoln last month and I heard that they got kicked out of another school in Portland."

* * *

"Mia, Mia – are you still with us?"

"Huh?" I turned my head to Tara who apparently had been trying to get my attention. "So, Mia, what do you think?"

"Think about what?" I said.

"The dance, Luke said we should all go to the dance?"

I felt my heart flutter – a vampire heart flutter that is. I wanted to go to the dance. Both Tara and I had been changed last year and since then we hadn't done much of anything fun. "Yes, I'd love to go."

Luke burst out laughing. "Yes, it will be like going to a dance and dinner – we can call it buffet night at the dance."

Matt turned his head to Luke. "You'd better cool it Luke, or we're going to get kicked out of this school too and I don't want to have to find fake parents again to meet with that goofball principle. We agreed to keep a low profile here and just kick back and enjoy ourselves – like we planned, remember?"

"Since when do you give the orders Matt? Don't forget who runs this group, if you don't like it you can leave at any time."

Matt saw Luke's eyes glowing red and backed down. "Sure, Luke, like the last guy that left, in pieces?"

I heard the bell ring and Darla looked over at Tara and me. "We all have to separate to go to classes you two don't do anything stupid – you know I can read your thoughts."

Tara followed me out of the cafeteria. "Mia, do you really think she can read our thoughts?"

I stopped walking for a moment. "She hasn't been able to so far, so I don't really think that she can, she's full of it." I could tell that everything was starting to get to Tara.

"Mia, I want to leave them and I know that Dorian is scared too why don't we just make a run for it?"

"I am working on it Tara, I'll figure out a way for us to leave and we will take Dorian with us, but for now lets just go along with them."

"Ok, Mia."

4

NOSEY NEIGHBOR

I stood out in the front yard of our home wearing my gardening attire, a pair of tan kaki jungle shorts and matching jacket and straw hat. I had just been ready to pick up the hose to water my plants when all of a sudden, I got an uneasy feeling. I paused momentarily and caught a whiff of something in the air, just for a split second as it blew by me, but I couldn't identify the scent. Whatever it had been it alerted my senses and they heightened. "You are just being foolish", I told myself and picked up the garden hose and started watering the enormous beds of Victorian annuals and perennials that covered our front yard. "That's it, drink up...I know you are thirsty", I told my little community of flowers while I watered them. Just then I'd heard a voice call to me from across the fence.

"Hello, yoo-hoo."

I turned my body around with the hose still in my hand and I saw a short elderly lady with grayish brown hair standing on the other side of the black-wrought iron fence that separated our yard from our neighbor's yard. I dropped my hose and took off my gardening gloves and let them drop to the ground and then I approached the fence line. She looked like she was in her late fifties and had petite features and small round blue eyes. "Hello, I am Antoinette Von-Allenberg", I said and extended my hand out to shake hers.

She shook my hand. "Hello, I am Mrs. Wanda Crabitz, nice to meet you."

She wasn't smiling and had a peculiar look on her face. "Is something wrong Mrs. Crabitz?"

"Well, yes dear, I am sorry to have to complain on our very first meeting, but I am afraid that I must."

"Yes, what is it Mrs. Crabitz?" I said and wondered what had been wrong.

"Well, it's about all of the young kids that I have seen around your house lately."

"All what kids?" I was surprised by her comment and wondered who she could possibly be talking about, other than Emma and her family who'd visited us over a month ago, we had no company, except for Ariel."

"Well, Mrs. Von-Allenberg…"

I interrupted her. "Please call me Antoinette."

"Ok, Antoinette and you may call me Wanda. It's those boys that I've seen outside your house late at night."

"I am sorry Wanda I don't know what you are talking about, it's only my brother and I that live here."

"Oh, then what are those boys doing outside your house and in your yard at all hours of the night?"

"I am not sure Wanda, but thank you for letting me know about it." I watched while she raised an eyebrow. The look on her face showed skepticism and it had appeared that she did not believe what I'd told her.

"Well, Antoinette I saw one of the boys walk right into your house, right through that front door."

"When did this happen, Wanda?"

"It was last week, around lunch time."

"Well Alexander and I would have been at work, and the house should have been locked up, I will let my brother know about this."

"Well I am only concerned because several houses in our neighborhood have been broken into and robbed and this is not the type of attention we want to draw to the neighborhood."

"Are you suggesting that Alexander and I are drawing this type of attention to the neighborhood, thieves or criminals?"

"Well, no but you're the youngest kids on the block, who else would those boys be visiting? I mean I saw them in your yard and in your house. We don't want any parties or loud music or any goings on like that. Mr. Crabitz and I don't have many visitors, anyway I thought you should know it's not the kind of thing we want in this neighborhood and I'd hate to have to call the police."

I understood why she didn't have many visitors she was not the most pleasant person that I had ever encountered. "If you do see anyone entering our house, especially on a weekday when we are at work please call the police!"

Just then I saw an elderly man walk out of the house and approach us. He was about the same age as Wanda and was short, balding and stout with a round midline. I assumed he was Mr. Crabitz. He stopped and stood next to Wanda and then looked at me directly. "Hello, I am Mr. Crabitz I hope Wanda is not bothering you?"

I watched while Wanda raised her eyebrows at her husband. "Albert how dare you say such a thing?"

I ignored their discussion. "Hello, Mr. Crabitz I am Antoinette Von-Allenberg, nice to meet you", I said and shook his hand.

Wanda turned back toward her husband. "I was just telling Antoinette about the young men that I have seen in her yard and at the house."

I could see the embarrassment in Mr. Crabitz's face. "Wanda their visitors are none of your business." Mr. Crabitz turned his head toward me. "I am very sorry Wanda gets a little carried away sometimes."

"No, that's fine, Mr. Crabitz, actually I am glad that she mentioned this to me, because whoever she had seen at our house were not visitors of – mine or my brother's."

"Oh, he is your brother I thought it was your husband."

"No, Alexander is my brother. But as I said, I am concerned that someone may have been snooping around the yard. Alexander and I are teachers at Lincoln High and we work during the days. Mrs. Crabitz just told me that she saw someone snooping around outside our home."

Mr. Crabitz turned back to his wife. "Ok, in that case Wanda, you are off the hook."

I watched while Wanda narrowed her eyes and smirked at her husband.

I looked at Mr. and Mrs. Crabiz. "Well, if you will excuse me I'd better get back to my yard work, thanks again for the information", I turned and walked away. "There goes the low profile that Alexander and I hoped to keep. Wanda was going to be a problem and would be watching our house twenty-four seven", I thought.

* * *

I sat in the living room of our house with Antoinette and I had been trying to put her mind at ease about her conversation that she had earlier with Mrs. Crabitz. "Antoinette, do you really believe the next door neighbor saw someone snooping around outside and that she actually saw someone walk into our house, or do you think she could be making it up?"

"Why would she make up something like that?"

"I don't know, maybe she's crazy, you did say she acted rather peculiar."

"Yes, she did act peculiar and then when Mr. Crabitz came out into the yard the very first thing that he had asked me was, "If she were bothering me?" But it's more than that Alexander when I had first walked out into the front yard and before Wanda had come out of her house I had caught a whiff of something, a scent - just for a brief second and its been bothering me all day its like I've smelt it before but I just can't put my finger on it."

I looked over at Antoinette and knew that she was upset, a scent to a vampire was important it was how we hunted and protected ourselves. "Just relax you will remember what it was."

"Yes, but that usually doesn't happen to me, I mean out of the five senses, sight, hearing, taste, touch and smell, you think that I could remember just one of them?"

I laughed. "You will remember Antoinette, it will come to you." All of a sudden Antoinette jumped up from the couch.

"Alexander, I remember the scent, its Luke's – Luke has been in our yard."

I didn't doubt my sister's abilities so I was sure that Luke had been in our yard. I knew that Luke was bad news, but I never expected him to come here, to our home. "What possible reason could he have to come here?"

Antoinette sat back down on the couch. "I made him angry, in class remember?"

"Yes I do, but why would he come to our house over something that trivial?"

"I don't know Alexander but he's pretty wicked."

"Ok Antoinette, if you are sure that he was here, then we need to be extra careful. He's trouble and I don't trust him. I will have an alarm system installed tomorrow so at least we won't have to worry while we are at work."

"Thanks, that sounds like a good idea."

"Antoinette until we figure out what's going on I don't want you going off anywhere by yourself, I mean it, there are seven of them and one of you. I know that you are really fast and can fight really good – I've seen you fight, but you are no match for seven vampires do you understand me."

"Yes, Alexander."

* * *

Two days had passed since Luke had visited our house and I lay in my bed thinking about everything, "Maybe Mrs. Crabitz had exaggerated and Luke had only been to the house once", I thought or at least that's what I hoped. I glanced over at the clock that hung on my bedroom wall it read eleven p.m. and I knew that

Alexander was still hard at work in his medical clinic doing research. I heard a knock on the door. "Who would be coming to our house this late", I wondered and got up and walked out of my room and down the staircase to answer the door. As usual, when I'd reached the last set of stairs instead of walking down them I slid down the banister, my inner child ruled! I landed on my feet in the foyer and straightened my body up and put on my serious face to answer the door. When I opened the door I was glad I did, a uniformed police officer stood in the doorway of our home.

"Yes, Officer, can I help you?"

"I am looking for Mr. Alexander Von-Allenberg or Ms. Antoinette Von-Allenberg?"

"I am Ms. Von-Allenberg, may I help you?"

"Is, Mr. Von-Allenberg at home also?"

"Yes, he is, he's my brother, what's this all about Officer?"

"Well, we've received a complaint from one of your neighbors about a party and some loud music coming from your home."

I laughed. "What? Well obviously there is some mistake, my brother is upstairs on his computer, I was in my room reading, and as you can see it doesn't appear that there is a party going on. There are no cars in the driveway or parked out front."

"Yes", he said and tilted his head sideways in an attempt to get a look into the house.

"Would you like to come in Officer?"

"Sure", he said and stepped inside.

Once he was inside, I watched his eyes scan the house. "What a nice house."

"Thank you, my brother and I are both doctors as well as teachers at Lincoln High School, we lead a relatively quiet life, so I can assure you there is no party going on here and probably never will be."

He smiled. "Well, Ma'am I am sorry to have troubled you, it's just that we have to respond to a complaint when it's called in."

"I understand, no worries, and Officer I am not trying to pry into your business, but I would assume it had been Mrs. Crabitz, next door who might have called you, she's been fairly rude to us on occasion."

"Well, thanks for that information Ma'am", he said and then left. I closed the door just as Alexander had come down the staircase. "Who was that?"

"It was the Portland Police Department, apparently our next door neighbor Mrs. Crabitz called in a complaint about a party and loud music coming from our house."

"Are you serious?"

"Yes, that's what the Officer said."

"You see Antoinette, she is crazy after all."

"Oh, Alexander between Luke and his gang and Mrs. Crabitz, I don't think this semester is going to be boring at all!"

5

SCHOOL DANCE

Alexander and I walked into – the gym. "Wow, Alexander the student committee did a really great job in decorating the gym for the dance."

"Yes they did the school colors of black and red look great. Look at the banner for the band and the black and red ribbons strung across the ceiling of the gym that must have taken them a long time to do."

"Yes, I am sure it did." I glanced around the gym and saw several long fold-out tables that sat against one side of the gym wall that held all the food and drinks. I watched while Alexander's eyes scanned the gym and I knew that he was looking for Ariel. She had also volunteered to be a chaperone for the dance. I saw Alexander's eyes light up when he saw Ariel. He looked over at me. "Antoinette, I will be back in a minute I am just going to run over and say hello to Ariel."

"I'll be here", I said and moved over near the gym wall. Just then Principle Hines walked up.

"Hello, Antoinette, I am on my way home and making some quick rounds to thank the teachers for volunteering to be chaperones, thanks again and please tell Alexander thank you also."

"No problem, Sir and have a good night."

Principle Hines left and a few minutes later Alexander returned. I smiled at him. "So did you get your Ariel fix for the night?"

"Funny, Antoinette."

"Principle Hines stopped by a moment ago to thank us for volunteering as chaperones."

Alexander smiled at me. "Principle Hines – has been great to work for."

"Yes, I agree, so how is Ariel doing?"

"Ariel and Mrs. Walters – the English teacher, are watching the students over in the left corner of the gym. Principle Hines wants two teachers in each corner of the gym so there are eight of us here tonight."

I listened while the band played they were set up in the far right corner of the gym. "They are not bad for a high school band."

Alexander looked distracted. "Antoinette, look who just walked in."

I turned my head and saw Luke and his friends, walk through the door of the gym. Luke and Darla were hand in hand, Matt and Jason were behind them and Mia, Tara and Dorian walked in last. "I hope they are just here to have fun", I said and exchanged glances with Alexander.

"We'd better keep an eye on them. I don't want you approaching them tonight without me, understand."

"Yes Alexander."

* * *

"Mia, it looks great!" Tara said as we walked into the gym. I looked around.

"Yes, the school colors red and black look awesome, everyone is dressed up, everyone but us", I mumbled.

Tara pointed to the banner that hung over the band. "Mia, look which band is playing."

I looked up and read the banner "Broken Glass", "Yes, Tara, they are good for a high school band." Luke, Darla, Matt and Jason walked ahead of me and then stopped alongside one of the gym walls. Tara, Dorian and I caught up with them and stood next to them for a moment. Luke, Darla, Matt and Jason then moved about ten feet away from us and huddled together talking.

* * *

Joseph, Mirka and I stood alongside one of the gym walls.

Joseph turned to face me. "Hey Lauren, look who showed up for the dance, it's that guy Luke and his friends from our vampire class."

"Yes Joseph, I see them, do you have them in any of your other classes?"

"No, I don't. Have you heard anything else about them?"

"Not much Joseph." I turned to Mirka. "How about you Mirka, do you know anything about them?"

"I know that a lot of the students don't like them. I remember what that feels like, when I first came from Russia my English wasn't good and some of the kids treated me pretty rough."

"Yes, I remember that Mirka, why don't you wave at them", Joseph said.

"Sure, ok." I waved at them.

"See that wasn't so bad, that one girl waved back, I think her name is Mia", Joseph said.

"You are such a coward Joseph, now I see why you wanted me to wave, you like Mia."

"No way, Mirka I just wanted to be nice and make them feel welcome."

* * *

Tara – looked over at me. "Who just waved at you Mia?"

"Those kids from our vampire class, Mirka, Lauren and Joseph."

"That's cool", Tara said.

"Yes, it is." I looked at the band while they played. It felt so good to just chill and listen to music without having to worry about Luke and Darla hovering over us or killing someone. Listening to the music brought back some memories of my life when I'd been a human.

"Tara, don't you miss being human?"

"Yes, Mia I do and I wish we were still back in foster care."

"Yes, I was happy, I mean before my parents died in the plane crash and before I went into foster care."

"But, that's where we met."

"Yes, and that's where we ran away from. Don't you ever think that if we hadn't run away that we would still be human now."

"Don't think about it Mia, we can't change what happened, I mean how could we have known what would happen."

"I know, and how could we have possibly known that hooking up with Luke and the others would have been such a disaster." Tara remained silent. I looked around the gym it was packed. The dance was for all grades, ninth through twelfth and the kids that weren't dancing stood in groups around the tables of food and others stood lined up against the walls of the gym.

Tara turned to me. "Mia look, there's that girl Melissa, the stuck up chick from our vampire class standing with that group of jocks."

* * *

"Shut up Melissa."

I looked at Erin standing next to Levi and David. "You shut up Erin."

Erin laughed and turned toward me and then tilted his head sideways toward the door. "Hey Melissa, take a look who showed up, it's Luke and his friends."

"Yes, I see them Erin. Who are those two guys that are always with Luke, do you know their names?"

"No, Melissa I don't" but Levi might. "Hey Levi do you know their names?"

"Yes they are Matt and Jason and I heard that they want to play football with us."

"Not as long as I am captain of the team. Hey Levi, one of them is staring at us, why don't you give him a Lincoln High welcome?"

"Ok Erin, here goes."

Erin and Levi were acting childish. I watched while Levi raised his hand and then started to extend his middle finger. I slapped his hand down.

"Ouch, that hurt Melissa."

"Too bad, knock it off before you start something", I said.

"Melissa, we aren't afraid of them, there are three of us and three of them."

"No Erin, there are four of them if you count that small dude."

"Ok Melissa, three and a half of them."

"Whatever, Erin they shouldn't even be here, one of you should go over and tell them to leave. Look at how they are dressed, they look like they just walked out of a subway, torn jeans and black t-shirts and tattoos and what's up with their eyes - it looks like they wear contacts."

"Give it a rest Melissa, sometimes I swear you think you own the school", Erin said.

"Let it go Melissa", Levi said.

"Erin you are my boyfriend you are supposed to be on my side. I see how it is? It is ok for you two to talk about them, but I can't. That girl Mia reminds me of that girl Emma from last semester, there was something strange about Emma and there is something strange about all of them too."

Erin turned to face me. "Oh I don't know Melissa, Mia is much prettier than Emma was."

"Shut up Erin."

"You are so jealous Melissa."

"I hate you Erin", I yelled while he walked away from me toward the restroom door.

"Relax Melissa Erin's just yanking your chain", Levi said.

I turned to Levi. "You both are supposed to be tough jocks, go over and tell them to leave."

"Melissa, we already sent them a message and I don't think they liked it, Luke hasn't stopped staring at us."

"What's the matter Levi are you scared?"

"No Melissa."

"Well, they don't scare me I am going over to tell them myself."

"Melissa don't go, wait until Erin gets back."

* * *

"Tara, this is awesome."

"Yes it is Mia I wish we could have fun like this all the time."

I looked over at Dorian. "You stay close to Tara and me? I don't know what Luke has planned for tonight, but I am sure he has his own reason for coming to the dance."

Dorian looked back at me. "Ok, Mia, I will."

Tara turned to me. "Hey, Mia, don't look now but it's that girl Melissa, she is walking toward us."

I turned around and watched while Melissa walked up and stopped right in front of me.

"Hello Mia"

"It's Melissa right?"

"Yes."

"So, Mia, why are you guys here?"

Melissa's question took me by surprise. "What do you mean?"

"I mean, why would a bunch of loser's like you guys even show up here and ruin the dance."

"Great, just what we need, trouble", I thought. "Melissa, I think it's best if you just turn around and leave."

"Yes, I bet you would like that."

Out of the corner of my eye I saw Darla looking over at us and then she moved toward us. I knew that if Melissa didn't get out of here now there would be trouble. I wanted one night of fun and no trouble.

"Melissa, you need to leave now, you can insult me another day." She didn't move.

All of a sudden Darla was at my side.

"Is there any trouble here Mia?"

"No, Melissa was just saying hello, she's in our vampires class, remember?"

Melissa smirked at me and rolled her eyes and then looked at Darla. "Well actually I was just telling Mia how I thought that you loser's really shouldn't be at the dance dressed like this, you all look like you walked out of a subway."

Darla half smiled at Melissa. "Listen you pathetic little cabbage-patched faced-troll, you'd better turn around and leave before I splatter you all over this nice clean floor."

"Darla, lets just go, she's not a problem."

"Shut up Mia if you know what's good for you."

I knew better than to push the issue any further with Darla. Melissa looked shocked and it was obvious that she didn't expect that response from Darla. The color drained from her face and she turned and walked away. I watched while Darla laughed hysterically and then exchanged glances with Luke who had looked over to see what was going on. She walked over to Luke and whispered something in his ear. I had a really bad feeling about tonight!

* * *

Alexander and I stood alongside the wall of the gym and I saw Ariel walking toward us. She stopped and stood next to Alexander, she turned her head toward me. "Hello Antoinette, how are you doing?"

"Fine Ariel, are you enjoying the dance?"

"Oh, Yes, I just love volunteering for things like this, anything to help the kids."

I smiled at Ariel and then watched while Alexander put his arm around her. "Ariel, would you like to dance?"

"Sure Alexander."

I escorted Ariel out and onto the dance floor and then took her into my arms and we began to slowly dance.

I put my head on Alexander's shoulder. "This is really nice Alexander." I followed his lead as we moved in a slow circular pattern with our bodies pressed tightly together. I had never felt as safe as I did now in his arms in my entire life and I was completely engulfed in the moment. The music ended and I looked up into Alexander's face while he looked down at me and then he kissed me. When we parted we walked off the dance floor and back over to Antoinette. "Thank you Alexander, that was nice."

"You are welcome Ariel."

Alexander and Ariel stood next to me. I tried to get Alexander's attention but he had ignored me. "Alexander, I am going to walk around and stretch my legs." He didn't respond and it appeared that I was invisible whenever he was with Ariel. I walked away from them and over to the other side of the gym and stood for a moment. There were students everywhere, laughing, talking, and dancing. I liked to see kids happy like this. Out of the corner of my eye I saw Luke and Darla and their group standing about thirty feet away from me. It was Luke's thoughts that had grabbed my attention. I could tell that he intended to harm someone. I followed his eyes around the room and they stopped on Melissa and Levi. They just walked out of the gym and it was obvious to me that they had been drinking. I watched while Luke and his group walked out after them. I thought about walking back across the gym to get Alexander, but there wasn't time. I followed behind Luke but had lost them momentarily. My instincts led me to an older part of the school and into an old gym. Once I entered it I saw that it was being used as a storage room for sports equipment. There were volley ball nets, poles and boxes of balls and other types of sports equipment stacked alongside the walls. It was dark except for the two exit signs that hung above the doorways. I saw Melissa and Levi standing on the top row of a set of bleachers near a huge glass window and they were taking turns drinking from a small glass bottle. "Great, I followed two kids from the dance in here so that they could sneak a drink", I thought. All of a sudden one of the gym doors opened and Luke and his friends entered the gym and leapt instantly to the top of the bleachers and surrounded Melissa and Levi. It had happened so fast that by the time I leapt to the top of the bleachers Luke had pushed Melissa and Levi through the glass window of the gym. The drop down was almost a one story fall but I knew they were dead even before they went out the window. Luke stepped toward me and I turned and leapt down to the gym floor. They followed me, and instantly surrounded me.

Mia stepped closer to Luke. "Come on Luke, lets get out of here, she's like us, she won't say anything."

I knew that Mia was making an attempt to save my life and the severity of my situation hit me hard. I heard Alexander's words-ringing-in-my-head, "Antoinette, don't do anything dangerous you are no match for seven vampires."

Luke moved toward me with his fangs fully extracted and I felt my fangs extract and the hairs on my neck stand up.

"So, look at what we have here – the pretty little vampire teacher all by herself, where's that little brother of yours to save you?"

"You're the one that's going to need saving", I told him, but knew that my display of bravery would not have any effect on him - he knew the odds as well as I did.

I looked at the rest of them Darla, Matt, and Jason they took a step toward me in a crouched position. "Could I out run them", I wondered. I had always been really fast, but some how I didn't think that I could outrun all seven of them and before I had a chance to react Luke lunged at me and grabbed me by the arm and threw me across the room. I hit the bleachers a good thirty feet away from where we had been standing and felt my body drop to the floor. I stood up. Darla, Matt and Jason were just about ready to leap forward when Luke screamed out at them. "No, she's mine back off."

They did as he said. I was glad. It would just be Luke and I for the moment, "If I killed Luke, would the others just leave", I wondered. I knew that probably wouldn't be the case, Darla would be out for instant revenge. Luke moved toward me again at top speed and I dodged him by jumping up into the air and landing ten feet away from where I had stood, I quickly turned to face him. He moved toward me again and I tried to dodge his charge a second time but he'd caught me by the arm and tightened his grip and then swung me around. "Nice try teacher, but you don't get an A you get a D for dead."

"Kill her Luke", Darla yelled in the background.

All of a sudden the double-wide doors of the gym burst open, I mean it looked like a tornado blew them open and both the doors broke off the hinges and fell to the floor. I watched while two really tall vampires entered the room at warp speed, it was like they were floating through the air. They moved with such preciseness that it was uncanny and unlike anything that I have ever seen before. Both vampires wore long black duster jackets, vests, jeans and black motorcycle boots with chains wrapped around them, their skin was vibrant and shiny, a little more than most vampires. The taller one had black mid-length hair and dark piercing black eyes and the second one had dark brown hair and green eyes. They stopped right along side me and I turned my head and looked at the tall vampire, his eyes met mine and I knew that they were here to help me.

The taller vampire turned to Luke. "Take your hands off her."

Luke released his grip on me and I immediately felt that Luke was afraid of them and I wondered if he knew them. Darla, Matt, Jason, Mia, Tara and Dorian immediately sped to Luke's side and surrounded him with their fangs extracted and remained in – a crouched position ready to fight.

Luke regained his confidence and looked at the tall vampire. "What's she to you?"

I watched while the tall vampire extracted his fangs and his eyes darkened and then his friend extracted his fangs and both vampires glared at Luke and the tall vampire spoke.

"If you don't turn around and leave, I am going to show you what she is to me."

I could tell that Luke didn't want to fight them, even with the seven in his group, he probably knew that he couldn't count on Mia and Tara and Dorian and that just left him, Darla, Matt and Jason, his four against the three of us, me and the two vampires who had just showed up to rescue me.

Luke slowly backed away. "Come on everyone, lets get out of here, I am bored."

I watched while Luke and his friends walked out of the gym. Now I was left with two vampires who I didn't know. I turned back around to the tall vampire. "Who are you?"

"I am Zackary William Bonney and this is my best friend and like-brother, Jeremy Jesse James, he goes by Jeremy and I go by just Zack."

It took me a minute to process what he had just said but then I got it, "As in Billy the Kid and Jesse James?" I asked.

"Yep, that's us."

"Like the real Billy the Kid and Jesse James?"

"Yes Ma'am in the flesh, vampire flesh that is."

I watched while they turned to walk away. "Wait, where are you going? I haven't even thanked you yet."

Zack turned back around. "No need to thank us –this is what we do – it's our thing, rescuing beautiful women, we'll be around if you need us again Antoinette."

"Wait, how do you know my name?" I watched them silently float through the air with speed and precision as they left the gym. I knew that Melissa and Levi were dead and that when their bodies were discovered it would look like two drunk kids who fell through the glass window of the gym. I needed to get back to the dance and find Alexander he would know what to do.

* * *

"Zack, why did you tell her that we were Billy the Kid and Jesse James?"

"I was just messing around Jeremy it's partly true, though we did ride with them."

"Yep Zack, those were some good days back then, but still that wasn't too cool, lying to her."

"I'll set her straight the next time we see her, I have a feeling we'll meet up with her again."

"So, Zack are you ready to start patrolling the clubs downtown? I am sure there is more than one woman in distress tonight who needs our help, a human who can't fight as well as Antoinette."

"Yes, she was pretty amazing the way that she faced seven vampires all at once."

I looked over at Zack. "Dude, if I didn't know you better I'd say you had a thing for her" I said and then we both laughed and ran warp speed into the darkness.

* * *

I returned to the dance and found Alexander standing in the same spot where I had left him. I walked toward him. "Antoinette, where have you been?"

I didn't answer him right away.

"What's wrong?"

I knew that Alexander was going to be really, really mad at me. "I know you are going to be really mad, but just listen?"

"Alright, what's wrong?"

"I followed Luke and his friends out of the dance, they were after two students. I followed them into an older gym but I was too late to stop them, they killed two students and then Luke pushed them through a glass window. It was two kids from our class Melissa and Levi. Mia tried to stop Luke but then he attacked me."

"Are you ok?"

"Yes."

"I warned you to stay away from them, I feared that they would be trouble, but I never thought that he would be brave enough to attack you."

"Well, there's more, when we were fighting, these other two vampires showed up."

"What two vampires?"

"I don't know they just appeared and helped me, they were amazing. They were tall and moved unlike anything I've ever seen before, with such precision and they chased Luke and his friends off."

"And you don't know who they were?"

I looked at Alexander and knew that my answer would sound ridiculous. "They told me that they are Billy the Kid and Jesse James."

"Are you serious?"

"That's what they said, but there's something else, Alexander, the taller vampire knew my name."

"Did you ask him how he knew your name?"

"I did, but he didn't answer me. The only thing I can think of is that he is like me I mean that he can read thoughts. He could have read Luke's thoughts."

"Well Antoinette, anything is possible it really could be Billy the Kid and Jesse James. I am upset with you though, you could have been killed tonight. What do I need to do to make you listen to me?"

"I am sorry I will never do anything like that again. I was really scared when I had to face all seven of them, if it hadn't been for Zack and Jeremy showing up I would have been dead for sure!"

"Well, I bet Luke will show up for class like nothing is wrong. I am going to have a talk with him tomorrow and set him straight. We can't control his hunting activities that's, for sure, but if he ever starts anything with you again I will finish it."

I hadn't seen Alexander this angry in years and I knew that he could take Luke, Matt and Jason out all at the same time but I hoped that it wouldn't come to that. Alexander and I hoped to reach young vampires just like Luke and his friends and show them that they didn't have to live like this anymore and that they had alternatives!

6

CLASS MEETS AGAIN

I sat next to Alexander and Ariel in the auditorium of the Drama Department, the school had been closed yesterday in observance of Melissa and Levi's deaths. I turned my head toward Ariel. "I wonder what Principle Hines wants to talk to us about?"

Ariel looked over at me. "I heard that – the police talked with some of the teachers and students and that the death's were ruled an accident."

"Yes, I heard that too they said the students were drunk and fell through the window."

Principle Hines entered the auditorium and walked to the center of the room and stood at the podium. He flicked the microphone with his finger and then cleared his throat before he spoke. "This is a sad time here at Lincoln. In the history of our school we have never had anything like this happen. I wanted to talk to you to let you know that the police might have some additional questions. If they do, they may interrupt your classes to pull students out to question them. I would appreciate your cooperation and if you need my assistance at any point, please call me immediately. The old gym is roped off and is off limits to students and teachers."

I watched while Mrs. Walters who taught English raised her hand to get Principle Hines attention.

"Yes, Mary", he said.

"I heard that you were having more security camera's installed at the school?"

"Yes, Mary, thank you for reminding me about that. I am having some additional cameras and an alarm system installed in some of the vacant areas of the school, like that old gym. If there are no additional questions, you are all free to return to your classrooms."

We stood from our seats and walked out the doors of the auditorium and I stopped and waited while Alexander said goodbye to Ariel. I watched their kiss goodbye, it always looked unnecessary to me. Ariel left.

I looked at Alexander, "It must be hard to go through an entire morning without seeing Ariel, I mean until lunch time that is?"

"Funny, Antoinette, you just wait, someday you'll meet your mate."

I smiled. "Doubtful but well see." I followed Alexander to our classroom and he unlocked the door. We stepped inside and stood near the door to wait for our students to arrive. I knew it would be difficult facing Luke and his friends after what they had done and I realized that we couldn't control them or their feeding activities. Alexander looked over at me and smiled. "Don't worry I am going to set him straight."

"Ok, but destroying him isn't my first choice I wish there was a way we could help him."

"It's not my first choice either Antoinette."

"These are the kinds of kids that we hoped to be able to help."

"Antoinette, I don't think Luke wants our help."

"No but Mia, Tara and Dorian do, hopefully we can help them and then deal with Luke and the others later."

"I created him Antoinette, I created them all - it's my mistake, I made them killers and monsters."

I watched as Alexander tilted his head down. I knew that he would never forgive himself for causing vampirism, but he had worked hard over the years to undo his mistake and finally now we were making a difference with our work.

Alexander raised his head and looked over at me. "Have you ever wondered if all of the other myths and legends were true?"

"What do you mean Alexander?"

"I mean, what if other myths like, werewolves, or zombies, or even aliens were true?"

I shuddered at Alexander's words I never had considered that before. "What if he was right and we lived in a world full of creatures and monsters", I thought. I walked away from Alexander and over to my desk and sat down, today I would be working on some research papers while Alexander taught our class.

I stood by the door after Antoinette had walked away. I wanted to talk to Luke about his fight with Antoinette and let him know that if he ever touched her again that he would have to deal with me. I watched while the students arrived and took their seats. Luke and his friends arrived last and Luke stopped right in front of me. He glared at me and it took all of my strength to keep my fangs in place and to not jump on him, I hadn't felt this angry in a long time. He could have killed Antoinette the other night and I wanted him to understand that he needed to stay away from her. "Take your seat, Luke, I'll talk to you after class", I told him while staring him down.

He cocked his head sideways and smirked. The low vampire growl that stirred in his throat was undetectable to the rest of the class and I returned a growl with equal strength. I stepped to the middle of the room. "Good morning class." I heard a mixture of good mornings – good morning Alexander, Professor and Mr. Von-Allenberg. "Today I will start with the anatomy and morphology of the vampire and when I finish my lecture Antoinette will spend a few minuets recapping some of our information from our "Vampires 101" class. I walked to the black board and picked up a piece of chalk and scribbled on the board - A vampire's anatomy and then drew a chalk outline of the human body. "Now first let me remind you that what I am teaching you falls under mythology and not medicine and is based on my own personal research, analysis and conclusion. Let's start with the head of the vampire and work our way down. A vampire is very much alive, like a human and the brain fully functions, as a matter of fact a vampire's brain functions far exceed that of a human. The five senses known to mankind, sight, hearing, taste, touch, and smell are extremely heightened in the vampire. The vampire brain differs from the human brain in that - the human brain feeds off blood that circulates in the body, a vampire does not have an active vein system so the brain is fed by fresh human blood that is ingested - ingested is the key word here."

I looked at my students face's and saw that they looked confused. I looked at Luke and his friends, they looked amused. I thought that this would be a good time to clarify this point. "Alright, everyone please keep in mind this is a mythology class and the anatomy that I am teaching you is in theory only." Three of my students, Lauren, Joseph and Mirka, the girl from Russia seemed to take an active interest in the lecture and were taking notes. I continued, "As I said, the five senses, sight, hearing, smell, taste and touch are extremely heightened in the vampire. A vampire can smell blood from a long distance away as well as hear sounds at least a mile away. Are there any questions so far?" I saw a hand go up, it was Mirka. "Yes Mirka?"

"I was wondering how good a vampire's sight is, can they see really far?"

"Yes, about triple that of a human's vision." I continued my lecture. "Ok, moving on to the vein system of the vampire. Vampires don't bleed, anyone want to guess why?" It was a rhetorical question and I knew they would assume that vampires didn't have blood in their bodies but that wasn't entirely true and I wanted to make that distinction. I looked at my students and their faces were blank. A hand went up. "Yes, Joseph?"

"They don't have blood in their body right?"

"Yes and no Joseph. Vampires do not have an active vein system that allows blood to remain in their bodies. When a human is infected with vampirism, one of the first things to shut down is the vein system and the body also stops producing blood and starts craving it. When this occurs, the secondary system used to circulate blood and fluids, takes over, this is the lymphatic system." I saw another hand go up and I was surprised, it was Mia. "Yes, Mia."

"What is the lymphatic system?"

"Good question Mia, the lymphatic system is like another vein system and it runs on the outer edge of the body, kind of like this chalk outline that I drew on the black board. If you trace around the whole human body it is one continuous trail without a break from head to toe. It is like one big vein and it carries blood and feeds the body tissue and the brain directly."

Mia smiled. "That's really interesting, so what does that mean for a vampire?"

"It is how a vampire's body feeds the brain, when they drink blood it enters the stomach and is absorbed from the colon tissue into the lymphatic system. The heart is nearly shut down and does not circulate blood any-more, so the muscles serve as an internal pump and push the blood through the lymphatic system to the brain to feed it directly, so that a vampire feels full. But when the blood is gone, the vampire gets hungry, kind of like putting gas in the tank of a car, when it runs out you must fill it back up."

I watched the look on Luke's face he actually looked interested in what I was saying.

Mia spoke without raising her hand. "Oh, that makes sense."

"Yes, it does, the vampire's anatomy isn't all that dif-ferent from a human obviously a vampire was once hu-man. When a human becomes infected, with vampirism, they stop producing blood, their vein system shuts down, and then most of the internal organ's shut down. The brain, lungs, stomach and lymphatic system func-tions in order to keep the vampire alive. The rest of the organs, the heart, kidney's, bladder, liver, pancreas, gall-bladder and other organs shut down." I saw a hand go up. "Yes Mirka"?

"Does the heart stop beating?"

"Almost, Mirka, it still beats but it is such a faint beat that it is undetectable by any medical machinery that we currently have today. It is more like an electrical current or pulse than an actual heart beat." I saw another hand go up. It was Lauren. "Yes, Lauren?"

"So the other organs just die?"

"No, Lauren they don't die, they just lay dormant, like they are asleep."

I looked over at Luke and his friends they looked shocked by my statement. "The anatomy and morphology of the vampire is quite complex and that is why I decided to teach this class in two parts. Alright, everyone I am going to break here. Antoinette is going to talk to you for a while." I stepped back to my desk and sat down and then watched while Antoinette got up and walked to the center of the room.

"Hello class, I am going to talk to you briefly about the mythology of the vampire. We covered this information in our "Vampires 101" class but most of you were not in that class, so I want to do a recap. Alexander and I believe that vampires first surfaced during the eleventh-century. Between the eleventh-century and the fourteenth-century little was known about vampires and they kept an extremely low profile. During the fourteenth-century, after Columbus discovered America is when vampires started coming to America. The fourteenth-century was called the "Age of Enlightenment", that's when humans actively started hunting vampires, books had been written on how to hunt vampires that date during that period. This was also the time when "Vlad Dracula" or "Vlad the Impaler" was born, some of you may – have heard of him. Between the fourteenth-century and the seventeenth-century vampires gained – publicity and popularity, in the seventeenth-century the first modern vampire poem was written, "Der Vampire." Then after the Salem Witch Trials, the New England vampire panic occurred and vampires ran ramped on the East Coast, they spread out, all over the world and started their own covens. In the country of Bulgaria there are over one-hundred cases of bodies that have been discovered that date back to the fifteenth-century, these bodies had iron stakes driven through the hearts. Bodies like these were the result of vampire hunts that were active back then. There was a body found that dates from the sixteenth-century, of a female who had not only been staked through the heart but had a huge brick stuffed in the mouth, against the fangs. I saw one of my student's hands go up. "Yes, Lauren?"

"Why was a brick stuffed in the mouth?"

"Well, I am not sure our speculation is that it was meant to keep the jaw from retracting, back to its human form, like to be trapped in the vampire state after they had staked the heart as proof that she really was in-deed a vampire."

"Wow, that's amazing."

"And more recently, some children playing in a field on the west coast discovered a gravesite that dated from the sixteenth-century. The graves discovered were typical burials of that period but the archeologist team found some rocks on top of a coffin and the rocks were used as some type of identifier for the coffin. It con-tained a body that had been dismembered. The bones were taken to a lab for analysis and determined that the breaks and fractures occurred after the victim had died. There are other accounts in the eighteen and nineteen-hundreds where entire families died all of a sudden from some illness, but in the cases where one family member survived, this family member was thought to be a vam-pire. This stuff is real people do you have any questions so far?"

I immediately saw Luke's hand go up and had regret-ted asking my question. I was almost certain that he would make some type of smart remark. "Yes, Luke?"

"Well if everything you say is true Antoinette then, I think that people should be very afraid of vampires, es-pecially at night, when they hunt." Luke and his friends laughed.

I saw Darla's hand go up. "Yes, Darla?"

"If vampires do exist, then that means that they are immortal and rule! And can do whatever they want."

Her comment infuriated me. I didn't think it deserved a response, but I wanted to make a point. "Let's discuss that a minute Darla, ok? Just because someone is stronger than another human being, that doesn't give them the right to overpower or hurt that person."

Darla looked confused. "Yes, but in theory vampires need blood to survive, they have to feed?"

"Yes, Darla but we live in a civilized society don't you think that a vampire might find other ways to feed, instead of killing innocent people?"

Darla looked at me confused. "Like what should they do, kill selectively?"

My hope was to show her alternatives of obtaining blood. "Well, for a vampire that would be a place to start, to retain my own humanity, or to try to protect my own soul."

Darla looked confused. "What soul, vampires don't have a soul?"

All of a sudden the bell rang.

Luke jumped up from his seat. "Come on, lets get out of here, and take our souls with us?" they all laughed and left the classroom.

I stepped back to my desk and watched while Alexander stood from his desk and approached Luke before he could leave the classroom.

"Hey, Luke, I'd like to talk to you for a moment." Luke turned to face me.

"What's up Alexander?"

Luke's friends stopped directly behind him. His blatant disrespect for me was obvious and I had expected it. It took a great deal of restraint to keep myself in check, after all I was the teacher. "Luke, I will make this short and sweet, I really don't care about your feeding activities, that's your business but if you or any of your friends ever put your hands on Antoinette again I will dispose of you - do you understand me?" For just one split second I saw fear in his eyes and then it faded.

"Now, Alexander that's no way to talk to a student, even if I am a hundred and fifty years old."

"Luke, I am serious – I will take you out."

"Look, Alexander it's obvious that I'll never make your teacher's pet list, so save your idle threats. I am on my way to my next class, Greek Mythology and I know there's someone there that you care about very much, I have my eyes - on that little red-headed beauty of yours!"

I felt myself jump backwards away from Luke and I knew it was a subconscious effort to keep myself from ripping his throat out. "Luke, if you touch one hair on Ariel's head, I'll rip your head off."

"Relax Alexander, she's safe for now, I'll have to chat with you later, I'm late for class." Luke laughed and walked out of the classroom.

I walked up and stood next to Alexander, I could feel the anger radiating from him. I knew that Alexander could kill Luke without much effort. He and I were older than other vampires and had a lot of experience fighting, we fought with the Roman soldiers, the Celtic warriors and the Britains in old England. "Well, that went well Alexander."

"He shouldn't have threatened Ariel, like that."

I turned my head toward my brother. "If a vampire truly had no soul then Luke would be my example, he is a ruthless killer and he has no intention of changing."

"I know Antoinette, what do your instincts tell you about them, who can we save out of that bunch?"

"Mia, Dorian and Tara are terrified and want to get away from them."

"Well then, we need to get them away from Luke as soon as possible!"

7

JEREMY AND ZACK

I sat crouched down next to Zack on the roof of Antoinette and Alexander's house. We had been watching their house off and on ever since we had helped Antoinette that night at the gym, when Luke had attacked her. Zack's premonitions had been getting stronger, he knew that something terrible was going to happen to Antoinette, but he didn't know when. He'd been like that, psychic even before we were changed to vampires, and his abilities had increased a lot more after we had been changed. I looked over at Zack. "It's pretty quiet out tonight."

"Yep, that's good though Jeremy I don't think Luke and his friends will be back tonight, I just wish I knew when."

"I know, me too Zack."

"Antoinette was in my visions even before we'd met her that night at the dance in the gym, you know how I am with the visions - I just go where they take us."

"I know", I said. I knew that there was more to it than just that. I had started to suspect that Zack had a thing for Antoinette, he was my best friend and we were changed at the same time. We actually did ride with Jesse James and Billy the Kid in eighteen-seventy-seven and that thought reminded me of the story that Zack had told Antoinette. "Hey, Zack you are going to have to tell Antoinette that we are not really Billy the Kid and Jesse James."

"I know, I was just messing around, but it probably wasn't the best time to be joking, I mean being in the midst of danger and all."

"Well, I am sure she will understand. What do you want to do? Should we sit here longer or should we go check out the clubs, they will be closing soon. I am sure there will be some girls in need of an escort home."

"Alright dude, let's head downtown. We can stop back here later."

Zack and I jumped from the thirty-foot rooftop and landed in the driveway and then we speed off for downtown Portland. We arrived at downtown Portland and stood under a light pole at the end of the street. This was a part of town where the popular clubs were that the college kids hung out at. It was Friday night and the clubs were packed. This position gave us a good view of an entire block and with our extended vision we could see the next two blocks as well. When the clubs closed and people started leaving we would be able to see any of the young women that left the club and looked like they were walking home alone. We usually watched to make sure that no one would follow them. It was crowded tonight, there were people walking by and just standing outside on the sidewalks talking and smoking and just hanging out. There was also a lot of traffic driving by.

"Hey, Zack, that guy over there is staring at us."

"I see him Jeremy he is probably just looking at how we are dressed."

"Yes, our duster jackets and black motorcycle boots always draw attention."

"Jeremy, he's walking over to us." I turned around and watched while the guy approached. I could tell that he was drunk.

"Who are you two supposed to be, it's not even Halloween. You look like cowboy gangsters."

He reached out and attempted to grab one of the chains that hung around my neck. I grabbed his hand

and pushed it backwards exerting a little too much force. I hadn't meant to push him that hard, he stumbled backwards to the ground and then got up. "Whatever, dude – no problem", he said and then turned and walked way.

People started walking out of the clubs and got into vehicles or cabs and some people began their walks home in groups. "Zack, look at all these drunks."

"Yep, I remember those days, sometimes I miss having a drink, how about you Jeremy?"

"You got that right I still remember that time after we became vampires when we tried to drink, that was the worst hangover in the world."

"Yes, we lost our whiskey and our guns when we changed, but we did gain hella speed and some awesome strength."

I laughed at Zack's comment and then pointed toward one of the clubs. Hey Zack look over there, those two girls who just walked out of that club."

"Yes, I see them, they are pretty wasted and they definitely shouldn't be walking home alone in that condition." One of the girls had red hair and was tall and the other girl was much shorter and had blonde hair. I watched while the blonde girl wobbled drunk down the sidewalk wearing a pair of four-inch spiked heels. They stopped and the girl wearing the heels put her arm out and leaned momentarily on her friend and adjusted her shoe strap. The girls continued walking and they didn't realize that there were three guys following them. Jeremy and I moved closer toward them and listened while they spoke.

"Wait up Kerilyn I can't walk fast in these heels, this sucks! I told you not to spend our cab money on those last drinks."

"Well, I told you not to wear those high-heels Ashley, take them off. It's not safe out here, and I want to get home while I can still walk. "

I turned back around to look at Ashley and noticed the three creepers about a block away. I felt an instant unsettling feeling in the pit of my stomach. "Hey Ashley, I think those guys are following us."

"Are you sure Kerilyn?"

"Yes."

I turned around to get a look at the guys myself and then took my heels off so that I could run faster. Kerilyn and I broke out in a run and Kerilyn ran ahead of me.

"Hurry Ashley, we've got three more blocks until we get to the campus."

"Wait up Kerilyn, they are catching up to us." I could hear the guys yelling out from behind.

"Hey baby, wait up, wait for us, we want to walk home with you."

Somehow I didn't think that was exactly what they wanted. "Wait Kerilyn, wait for me."

I couldn't leave Ashley behind so I slowed down until she caught up with me and then by that time, so did the guys. We stopped and the three of them surrounded us and circled us like a pack of coyotes.

"Hey, girls, we just wanted to talk to you for a minute" One of the guys reached out and grabbed Ashley's arm. I slapped at his hand. "Leave her Alone." He grabbed me by my hair and yanked it, and then from out of nowhere, two really tall guys appeared.

Zack and I sped alongside the girls. I grabbed the arm of the guy who held one of the girls by her hair and slapped his hand away from her. "Dude, that's no way to treat a lady."

He looked at me. "You two should mind your own business, we were just trying to walk them home", he said and then they all laughed.

I turned to the girls. "You girls know these guys?"

"No, we don't, they were following us, please help us."

"That's what I thought." Zack and I had no tolerance for any guy that didn't treat a woman with respect. I watched while Zack stepped really close to the guy and looked him right in the face.

"You three, leave, now."

"And who is going to make us?"

"I am." I felt my fangs extracting and I knew that my eyes were glowing red. "That ought to do it", I thought.

The guys backed away from me, one at a time and one of them stumbled to the ground. "What the hell are you?" he said and then got up and ran after his friends.

Before I turned around to face the girls, my fangs retracted and my eyes adjusted. "You girls shouldn't be walking alone this late at night, why don't you let Jeremy and I walk you home. I assume you are headed to the campus?"

"Yes, thanks I am Kerilyn and this is my friend Ashley."

I am Zack and this is Jeremy, glad we could help. We are just passing through Portland."

"Whatever dude, I am just glad that you were here now." I put my arm around Ashley she was crying. "It's ok these guys are going to walk us home."

8

NEIGHBORHOOD WATCH

My conversation with the neighbor, Mrs. Crabitz had not been going well! I had been out in my front yard watering my plants when she had yelled at me from across the fence. She accused Alexander and I of having a party at the house last night - and that's the note that our conversation had started on. I stood alongside the fence line looking at her. "Listen Mrs. Crabitz, I have been very polite with you up until now, but I must tell you that if you keep this behavior up and keep calling the police on us, Alexander and I will be forced to talk with the Police Chief and then with our lawyer." Just then I saw Mr. Crabitz walk out of the front door and into the yard, he approached us and apparently had heard what I had said. "Oh, Ms. Von-Allenberg, I can assure you that there will be no more problems."

Mrs. Crabitz interrupted him, "But Albert I saw some boys on the roof, just last night."

Mr. Crabitz turned to his wife. "Wanda it's a three story house with a high pitched roof and sharp dormers no one could walk on the top of that roof it's too steep. Next you'll be telling us that you saw Santa Claus."

"Albert, why don't you believe me, I know what I saw."

I turned back to Mrs. Crabitz. "Really, Mrs. Crabitz this has to stop. I do wish you would pay less attention to our house and watch your own house."

Mr. Crabitz looked at me. "Antoinette, it won't happen again, if she bother's you or your brother please let me know right away."

"I appreciate that Mr. Crabitz. I know that there have been some robberies in the area, but despite that, Mrs. Crabitz is taking it a little too far. She called the police last week and filed a false report that we had a party at the house and Alexander and I were the only ones home and the house was quiet. This is the behavior that we won't put up with. Alexander and I have formed a neighborhood watch and are patrolling the neighborhood in the evenings."

Just then Alexander walked out of our house and joined us in the yard. "Hello, Mr. and Mrs. Crabitz, I am Alexander Von-Allenberg", I said and held my hand out to shake their hands.

"Hello, I am Albert Crabitz, nice to meet you and this is Wanda, my wife."

"Yes, I've heard a lot about Wanda from Antoinette", I said and looked over at Mrs. Crabitz.

I looked over at my brother. "Alexander, I was just explaining to Wanda about how we would like her to stop interfering in our business, for a lack of better words."

"Yes, Mrs. Crabitz that would be most helpful, Antoinette and I lead a fairly quiet life as doctors and teachers and on occasion we visit with some patients here in the privacy of our home, so we would appreciate it if you would please respect our privacy."

Mr. Crabitz looked at Alexander. "Yes, Alexander that won't be a problem anymore, I've just told my wife to mind her own business."

I smiled at Mr. Crabitz and assumed for him that life was no picnic.

"So Alexander, your sister just told us that you have formed a neighborhood watch?"

"Yes, Sir that's my sister – the one woman police squad."

I hit Alexander against his ribcage with the back of my hand. "Funny, Alexander."

Alexander looked back at Mr. Crabitz. "We are going out tonight for a while, so if you see us coming and going during the night hours, please don't be alarmed we are just patrolling the neighborhood."

Mr. Crabitz smiled. "Well, that's very admirable of you both, we appreciate that and if I hear of anyone who wants to join I will send them your way."

"Thank you Mr. Crabtiz."

"Ok, Wanda lets get back into our house and mind our own business."

I looked at my brother and smiled and watched while Mr. and Mrs. Crabitz went back inside their house. "Alexander, what time do you want to go out tonight?"

"I thought we'd leave around midnight."

"Sounds good, I would also like to check out the school tonight I've had an uneasy feeling about it lately."

"Alright Antoinette, I would like to take a run over to the blood bank on Elm St."

"The blood bank, why?"

"It was broken into last night. Just before I came out into the yard the Director called to let me know what had happened and that someone got away with over fifty bags of blood."

I looked over at Alexander and knew that he was thinking the same thing that I was who else would want that much blood? No one except a, vampire. "Do you think that Luke had anything to do with it?"

"Well, he must have followed us home from school, because he knows where we live and he's been here, maybe he followed us to the blood bank? This is getting out of hand, first Luke was here at the house, he is running ramped at school and now he's broke into the blood bank. We have to stop them before anything else happens it's about time we started following Luke!"

* * *

I glanced at my watch, it was almost midnight and I just finished dressing to patrol the neighborhood with Alexander. I always believed in dressing appropriately for whatever endeavor lay ahead. I heard Alexander call out to me.

"Antoinette, are you almost ready?"

I smiled as I glanced at myself in the mirror. I wore a pair of black denim jeans, a black hoodie and a black stocking cap. I didn't know where our activities might take us tonight and I wanted to be ready. I was sure

Alexander's patience had expired. I had – been correct when I heard his voice ring out again from downstairs.

"Antoinette, are you ready yet?"

"Yes, on my way down", I yelled and then sped from my bedroom down the staircase. I got to the last set of stairs and slid down the banister and landed on my feet in the foyer and then straightened my body up.

Alexander stood by the door. "Are you sure that you are ready? Is that lipstick the right color for tonight?"

"Funny, Alexander, are you ready?"

"I've been ready for a while, let's go, it's almost mid-night." I followed Alexander out the front door and we walked down the street and then over to the next block. The neighborhood looked quiet we didn't see anything that looked suspicious. We moved one more street over and walked side by side.

"Antoinette, its pretty quiet out, lets head over to the blood bank on Elm and check it out." I knew that Luke and his friends had something to do with the stolen blood.

"Alexander, Luke is still killing to feed, what would he want with the blood from the blood bank? It doesn't make sense."

"My guess is that he's selling it to other vampires."

"Oh, I didn't think about that." We turned down the next street and then broke out into a run and it only took a few minuets to run the three miles to the blood bank.

We arrived at the blood bank and I stood next to Alexander in front of the small brick building. It looked deserted.

"Lets go around back and check it out, Antoinette."

I followed Alexander around to the back of the building and we stopped. All of a sudden I saw something out of the corner of my eye and I turned my head and looked down the side of the building. "Alexander, look it's Luke and his friends."

"I see them."

We moved to the right corner of the building and I stood behind Alexander. "Do you think that they saw us?"

"It doesn't appear so, what are they doing?"

"It looks like they are just coming out of that window."

"Lets move closer to them, Antoinette."

I followed Alexander down the side of the building they had their backs to us. It looked like they hadn't sensed our presence then all of a sudden they took off running.

"Let's go Antoinette." We followed them but kept a distance and it was obvious to me where they were heading. "Antoinette, it looks like they are heading toward the school." We stopped near the fence of the school grounds. "Stay back Antoinette."

"Did they spot us?"

"I don't think so, but let's just stay here for a moment."

I stood next to Alexander and watched while they took turns jumping over the fence onto the school grounds. Luke looked back for a second and paused, then led his friends into the maintenance building. "Well, Alexander, at least we know where they will be for a while. What if the blood is for them? Maybe they are trying not to kill."

"I would love to believe that Antoinette, but I really doubt it. I think he is selling it to other vampires."

"Yes, you are probably right."

"Antoinette, what time is it?"

"It's one-thirty a.m."

"What are they doing in there, why haven't they come back out?"

All of a sudden it hit me. "Alexander, I think they live here, on school grounds!"

9

MIA, TARA AND DORIAN

I sat at my desk in my medical clinic on the third floor of our home. My cell phone rang and I picked it up and hit talk.

"Hello, Alexander, how are you doing?"

"Hello Charles, it's good to hear from you, we are doing fine, how is everyone doing in Alaska?"

"Oh, just fine, we are so very happy. Eloise and I have adjusted beautifully to being human we are expecting a baby next spring. Lucy is dating a nice young man from the college that she attends and Emma and Taylor are engaged and planning their wedding for next spring and we owe everything to you."

"No more thanks are necessary, this is what Antoinette and I enjoy doing, helping to give vampires their human lives back. Please tell Eloise, Lucy and Emma that we miss them, especially Antoinette, she talks about Emma often."

"I will. I was calling to give you both an early invite to Emma's wedding, it is eight months away, but I know with your busy schedules I thought I'd better let you know as soon as possible. The wedding is June sixteenth and Emma would love for you both to attend, it will be here in Fairbanks. June is a beautiful month here and you both are welcome to stay with us at the house."

"Absolutely, Charles we will be there, I know that Antoinette wouldn't miss it for the world."

"So, Alexander how is your work going, have you helped any other vampires?"

"Well, not yet, but we did get a group of seven vampire kids in our class this semester. Three of them we hope to help, two girls and a young boy, but we are having problems with the other three vampires and their leader Luke. He is extremely difficult."

"You know Alexander, I've been thinking recently about how much you and Antoinette have given us, I mean, our lives back. I was thinking that maybe there is something else I can do to help, as a psychiatrist I mean. Maybe I could counsel some of the kids and Eloise and I could be a foster home for the kids who don't have the ability to live on their own."

"Charles, that is a fantastic idea, but you have already done so much. Both your monetary contribution and the home you donated to us – here in Portland are enough."

"Alexander, what are the ages of the kids?"

"Well I am not sure, the two girls look about sixteen and the younger boy around fourteen, but I am not sure when they were changed. They look very inexperienced, I mean as vampires so I am guessing they were recently changed."

"Well you let me know if Eloise and I can help with them, just give me a call."

"Thanks Charles I appreciate that and I'll keep in touch, I'll tell Antoinette about the wedding and we will see you then."

"Goodbye, Alexander"

"Goodbye, Charles." I hung up the phone.

* * *

Tara and I stood outside of the maintenance building and Luke and the others were still inside. I hated that we had to always tell them where we went. Luke wasn't afraid that we wouldn't return, Dorian was inside with them and if we didn't, we knew what they would do to him."

"Mia, maybe we should talk to Antoinette, maybe she and Alexander can help us?"

I looked over at Tara. "Keep your voice down or Luke will hear you, why would Alexander and Antoinette help us? They knew that Luke killed the students and they didn't do anything about it. You heard what Alexander told Luke that day, in class when he stopped him at the door – he said that he didn't care about his feeding activities and then warned him to stay away from Antoinette. I don't think they want to get involved in our problems." I watched while Tara put her head down she looked upset and I didn't blame her, I wanted to get away from Luke also.

"Ok Mia, I guess your right, but couldn't we just try anyway?"

"You know what Luke and the others will do to us if they find out."

"Yes, but I don't care anymore I don't want to live like this forever, I am so unhappy."

"I am too Tara. Alright, we will try and talk to Antoinette but we will have to find a way to meet with her alone, without the others knowing."

"Maybe we can write a note and drop it in the classroom and then she will find it."

"Tara, that's not a bad idea, but we would have to ask her to meet us here on school grounds, at night and we would only have a few minuets to talk to her, she might not come."

"I know, but let's try, please Mia. "

"Ok, Tara." Just then Luke, Matt, Jason, Darla and Dorian walked out of the building.

Darla walked up to us, "What are you two doing out here for so long?"

I looked at Darla. "You know, just soaking up the sun!"

Darla smiled. "Funny Mia you are just hilarious you missed your calling you should have been a comedian instead of a vampire."

"Is it too late to change my mind?" I asked jokingly.

Darla shot me a look of disgust. "Yes, sorry sweetie, it's just a little too late for you, let's go."

I looked at Darla and the others. "Where are we going?"

Luke turned his head toward me. "We are going downtown to the college campus to hunt for some fresh meat."

I looked at my watch, it was six o'clock in the evening and it was still light out but the brightness of sun had long faded. I hated hunting, but we had to eat. I survived on leftovers from the others.

We broke into a run and it only took a few minutes to reach the campus. Luke positioned us in a wooded area near the dorms. Now we would sit and wait, this was Luke's routine for hunting, he would wait until it got dark and then seek out his victims. This is what I hated about being a vampire!

10

CLASS MEETS AGAIN

It was Friday morning and Alexander and I just unlocked our classroom door and stepped inside. Alexander sat down at his desk, today he would be working on some medical papers and I would be teaching our class. I stood in the center of the room and watched while the students entered the room and took their seats.

"Good morning class."

I heard a mixture of replies, "Good morning, Antoinette, Mrs. Von-Allenberg and Professor."

"Today we have a guest speaker she will be arriving at any moment. Some of you may know her, Ms. Ariel Domande, she teaches the Greek Mythology class. Ms. Domande will be giving you a lecture on the Greek Myth of how vampires were created." I had just finished speaking when Ariel walked through the door. I turned my head to look at her, it had been pouring down rain all morning and her red hair was somewhat frizzed out.

Her five-foot, two-inch frame had been concealed under her huge raincoat and her big rubber boots made her look like a kindergartner whose mother had just dropped her off for school.

"Hello, everyone, I am sorry I am late."

I watched while Ariel removed her rain coat and then hung it up on the coat rack near the door. She removed her rubber boots and also left those by the door. She held a black notebook in her arms as she moved toward the center of the room. I stepped back to my desk and sat down and looked over at Alexander sitting at his desk, he was staring at Ariel and looked like a love sick vampire. I shook my head sideways at Alexander and then turned my head back toward Ariel and listened while she addressed the class.

"Hello, everyone, I am Ms. Domande, but you may call me Ariel and I am going to lecture to you on the Greek myth of how vampires were created. It all started back in Greece in a city called "Delphi" and the particular document that records this myth is called the "Scriptures of Delphi." The premise of the scriptures is that only a vampire can create a vampire, so logic would tell us that the history of vampires began with a single vampire. Delphi was home to the God Apollo, I am sure that most of you have heard of Apollo. The story goes like this – there was a man named Ambrogio who was from Italy and he wanted to have his fortune told at the Oracle of Delphini. The Oracle of Delphini was a temple and a fortune teller named Pythia served the temple. She was only known to say a few words to those whose fortune she told and her messages were usually cryptic. When Ambrogio visited her all she said to him was - The moon and the blood will run. Of course Ambrogio didn't understand what she'd told him and when he was leaving the temple he met Selene, a beautiful young virgin servant girl and they instantly fell in love."

Luke's hand went up immediately. I looked at Luke. "Yes, Luke?"

"Ariel, was this beautiful virgin girl at the temple as beautiful as you?"

Luke knew that Alexander and I were dating and I knew that he had asked the question intentionally. I turned my head sideways and I could see Alexander sitting at his desk, he looked angry.

Ariel looked back at me briefly while I sat at my desk behind her. Luke asked that question on purpose to make me angry, and it had worked. He knew that Ariel and I were dating.

Ariel turned back to Luke. "Why, thank you Luke, what a lovely thing to say, but no I am sure she was much prettier than I am. Ok, class as I was saying. Apollo got angry because Selene was his favorite servant and he cursed Ambrogio so that his skin would burn if he ever touched the sunlight. Ambrogio hid in the dark until one day he traded his soul to Hades, the God of the underworld. Hades told him he would break the curse so that Ambrogio could be with Selene, if he would steal the silver bow of Artemis, Apollo's sister, Ambrogio agreed. Artemis caught him trying to steal the silver bow and she also cursed him so that he could never touch silver. He was miserable but eventually Artemis took pity on him and gave him the gift of immortality and the gift of strength and speed and fangs to become a hunter. His skills were only second to hers. She took pity on him once again and told him that if he worshiped her forever that he could be with Selene. He agreed and he and Selene lived in a cave and worshiped Artemis together. Eventually Selene grew old and she was dying and Ambrogio begged Artemis to save her. Artemis told him to bite Selene on the neck and kill her and at first he didn't want to but Selene begged Ambrogio to do as Artemis said. He bit her and all of a sudden Selene began to radiate and glow with light and she was young again. They returned to Italy and lived and had children and became the very first vampire clan. So there you have it, the Greek myth about how vampires were created, are there any questions?" Luke raised his hand but before I could call on him Alexander stood from his desk and moved alongside me.

I turned my head toward Alexander. "Hello, Alexander, thank you for allowing me to share this story with your class."

"You are welcome Ariel, thank you for coming." We had been ignoring Luke while he had his hand raised in the air and finally he just blurted out his question anyway.

"Ariel, where did you get that beautiful red hair from, your mother of father?"

I could tell that Luke's question had upset Ariel, her parents had just passed away last year. I looked at Luke, "Luke, that's enough, if you don't have a question related to the subject matter of this class – don't ask it, is that understood?" He remained silent. I had embarrassed him in front of Ariel and the class and he looked angry!

The bell rang and the students began leaving the classroom. Luke paused at the door and turned back around and glared at me. I returned his stare while he walked out of the room.

I walked toward Alexander and Ariel. "Thanks Ariel, for the presentation I really enjoyed it."

"Your welcome Antoinette, thanks for having me, I love talking about Greek Mythology ...oh, wait, someone dropped this? Hey guys, you dropped this", I attempted to call out to Luke and his friends, but they had already walked out of the classroom. I bent over and picked up the small piece of paper it had been folded several times over to the size of a quarter. I opened it and read it and then I turned to Antoinette. "Antoinette, it is for you." I handed the note to Antoinette.

I took the piece of paper from Ariel and stared at it for a moment. I couldn't believe what was scribbled in ink on the paper "Please help us Antoinette, we need to talk to you, please come to the school tonight at ten o'clock and meet us outside of the maintenance building, please, Mia."

I handed the note to Alexander and he read it. "Antoinette, it could be a trap?"

"I don't think so Alexander, I think they really want our help."

I watched while Ariel turned her head toward Alexander. "Alexander, what's going on, what is the note all about?"

Alexander didn't answer Ariel right away – he exchanged glances with me and then I walked over and pulled our classroom door shut. I wasn't sure how much my brother had told Ariel about our work here. I stepped back toward my desk and sat down to give Alexander and Ariel some privacy. Ariel looked confused and she asked Alexander her question again.

"Alexander, what's going on?"

I turned toward Ariel. "Ariel, Luke and his friends are vampires, all seven of them." Ariel looked shocked.

"Oh, Alexander, are you sure?"

"Yes, Ariel I am sure Antoinette and I know a vampire when we see one, we recognize each other instantly. The three younger vampires, Mia, Tara and Dorian have been trying to get away from Luke and they need our help. Mine and Antoinette's, that's what we are doing here, trying to help young vampire kids."

Ariel looked confused. "Oh, Alexander, we really haven't talked about you...you being a vampire or your past."

I felt sorry for her, I had been completely unfair, I had held a lot back and hadn't told her that much about myself or Antoinette or our past and I knew that this was something I needed to rectify immediately. "Ariel, there is so much more that you need to know and I should have told you sooner. Can we talk tonight after school? Would you please come to the house and I will make dinner for you?"

"Yes, I would like that, what time?"

"Would you please just follow me home tonight after school?"

"Well, I'd like to go home first and change." I noticed the look on Alexander's face, something was wrong. "What is it Alexander, what haven't you told me?"

I didn't know how she was going to take what I had to tell her. "Ariel, its Luke, I am afraid he has his eyes on you."

I looked at Alexander. "What does that mean has his eyes on me? Like what - as a snack?"

"Yes I am afraid so, he is angry with Antoinette and I and our work has put you in danger."

"Oh, really Alexander, you don't think that he would actually hurt me? I am a teacher here and he is a student."

I watched Alexander and Ariel talk and he wasn't getting through to her. I stood from my desk and approached them and turned to Ariel. "Ariel, this is serious, Alexander is not kidding, Luke is after you and we are worried. Luke is a ruthless killer he is the one who killed those two students last week."

Ariel looked shocked. "What do you mean he killed them, I thought they were drunk and fell through the gym window while goofing off on the bleachers?"

"No, Ariel, I was there – I mean I got there too late just when it was happening. Luke killed them, pushing them out the window was only a way to disguise their wounds caused by the vampires."

"Are you for real, is this really happening?"

"Yes Ariel, now do you see why Alexander and I are so worried about you?"

I saw the seriousness on Antoinette's face and heard it in her voice. I turned to Alexander. "Ok, we will do it your way I'll follow you and Antoinette home after class tonight."

* * *

The day had ended and Antoinette and I stood in the parking lot next to Ariel's blue beetle waiting for her. I saw her approaching us.

"You guys ready to go?"

"Yes, we are Ariel."

I watched while Ariel's eyes scanned the parking lot. "Alexander, where did you park?"

"Right here", I said and pointed to the brand new black Hummer that sat parked next to her beetle.

"Wow, Alexander this is awesome you didn't trade in your 1939 Roadster did you?"

"No way, it is home in the garage, that car is a classic."

We walked over to the Hummer and Ariel looked inside through the window. "When did you get this? It's gorgeous."

"I ordered it online last week and they delivered it last night."

"I love it. It's just great I never rode in a Hummer before."

I stepped next to Ariel. "Do you want to ride home with me? I am sure that Antoinette wouldn't mind driving your beetle to our house."

"Had my brother completely lost his mind, did he actually just volunteer me to drive that roller skate?" I thought. He knew that I hated her car and despised how small it was. I watched while Ariel almost jumped up and down like a child.

"Oh, yes Alexander I would love to ride in it."

I looked at my brother and he looked at me with that please, I owe you look on his face. "Antoinette, you don't mind driving her car home do you?"

I smirked at Alexander. "Of course I don't mind, I would love to drive the little beetle home."

Ariel handed me her keys. "Oh, thanks Antoinette."

I took the keys and walked over to the bug and got in and started up the car. "Buckle up it's the law", I heard Ariel's voice ring out even though she wasn't here, but this time I didn't put my seat belt on. I drove behind the Hummer and followed them home.

We pulled into the house and parked the cars and I followed Alexander and Ariel up to the door. I waited while Alexander unlocked the door and we stepped inside and then Alexander entered the security code on the alarm pad.

Ariel looked confused. "Alexander, when did you put in the alarm?" She asked him.

"I had it installed a few days ago when our neighbor Mrs. Crabitz told Antoinette that she had seen someone in our yard late at night. I also had some surveillance cameras installed on the property because Mr. Crabitz told us that there have been some robberies in our neighborhood."

I turned around and looked at Alexander and Ariel. "I am going to go upstairs and get changed and give you two some privacy to talk." I knew that Alexander was worried about what he had to tell Ariel and how she would take it.

Alexander looked at me. "Thanks Antoinette."

I went upstairs and left Alexander and Ariel in the foyer.

After Antoinette left I turned around and faced Ariel. "Ariel, why don't we go into the kitchen, I am going to make you that dinner that I promised you." We walked into the kitchen. "Please, just have a seat and dinner will be ready in about a half hour."

"Can I help you cook?"

"Not necessary, I went to the supermarket, the one near the school between our classes – earlier today and got everything that I needed. So how does Pastitsio sound?"

"Oh, Alexander that's a Greek pasta dish, I love it."

"Well, one Greek dinner coming up."

"What time are you and Antoinette meeting with the kids tonight?"

"At ten o'clock, so we will leave here about nine-forty-five." I didn't want to tell her that it really wasn't a meeting, if the kids were ready to leave we would take them and hopefully without a fight. As I prepared the food I looked over at Ariel sitting at the kitchen table, she wore a turquoise turtle-neck sweater and a pair of dark denim jeans with her black high-heeled boots that she bought at the mall. Her pearl earrings and necklace looked great and she looked so refined and beautiful. I owed her an explanation about myself and Antoinette, it was long overdue.

"Alexander, are you sure I can't help you?"

"No, thank you I've got it", I said and continued preparing the food. "Ok, Ariel here goes, all about me – I was born in eleven-twenty-two A.D." I was worried how she might feel about my real age.

She looked shocked. "Wow, you are like almost nine-hundred years old."

"Yes, something like that, does that upset you?"

"Are you kidding, that's awesome, it's absolutely fantastic, oh, there's so much that I can ask you about and you have all the answers, the real answers because you were there."

She never ceased to amaze me, I just told her that I am almost nine-hundred years old and she found it awesome. "So, my age doesn't bother you?"

"No, way – it's too cool."

That was one of the things I loved about her, she was so very understanding. "Ok, one down, now the hard part", I thought. "Ok Ariel, in the eleventh-century I was both a physician and a scientist."

"How wonderful Alexander, you must know every thing about medicine from the very beginning?"

"Yes, Ariel, but I am afraid it goes beyond that?"

"Alexander, what do you mean?"

"Well, for starters, vampires."

"What about them?"

"I created them."

"What do you mean you created them?"

"Ariel, many years ago I was conducting a medical experiment in my lab, an experiment on myself and the experiment went bad. I gave myself a serious blood disease that wouldn't allow my blood to replenish itself and I turned myself into a vampire."

"Well, there is nothing you can do about it now, I am sorry that it happened but it was an accident."

She had amazed me again by shrugging off the fact that I had created vampires, horrible killing machines with no regard for human life. "Well, actually Ariel there is something I can do about it now, that is why Antoinette and I are here. My research and work all of these years has been directed at how to correct my mistake – I mean how to change a vampire back to being a human."

"Is that what you meant about helping vampire kids?"

"Yes, those who want to change back and want to be human again." Ariel looked surprised. "Ariel, are you ok so far, with what I am telling you?"

"Yes, Alexander it's just a lot to take in, I mean up until I met you I didn't believe in vampires. I thought they were a myth and now you are telling me that Luke and his friends are vampires. I mean they have been in my class for weeks now and I didn't even know that."

I strained the pasta noodles and then added them to the vegetable mix that was sautéing in the skillet.

"I know it's a lot to take in."

"How many other vampires are out there?"

"Lots, and usually they are wealthy and educated, but lately a lot of young vampires are breaking away from their covens and trying to start their own covens."

"Is that what happened to Luke, you think he used to belong to a coven of vampires."

"Yes, I am almost certain of that, but he's on his own now and trying to start his own group, he is sort of collecting vampires, that's what Antoinette believes anyway."

"Oh, that's right she can see things, like the future?"

No not really, she just reads thoughts, she can see the past if someone is thinking about it, or the future if someone is planning something, as long as it is a part of their thoughts."

"Oh, the food smells really good. Can Antoinette read both a human and vampires thoughts?"

"Yes."

I turned in my chair to face Alexander. "I still don't understand why Luke is after me?"

"Well, he doesn't like Antoinette or I and he might even suspect that we are interested in Mia, Tara and Dorian, or it may be that he is just attracted to you." I didn't want to tell her the rest of the scenario but I knew I must, she really needed to understand the severity of her situation. "Luke may not intend to kill you, he may want to change you."

"What do you mean change me?"

"Change you into a vampire." She looked scared. "Ariel, I am not sure exactly what his intentions are but I know that he is definitely after you. I have had some uneasy feelings about you lately and Antoinette has been having some visions about you."

"What kind of visions?"

"She is having visions about you being in danger."

"Now I am scared."

"Well don't worry I won't let him hurt you. But Ariel there is something else I need to tell you, about myself, before we go any further and if you don't want to continue our relationship I will understand."

"Don't say that Alexander."

"Ariel I have killed people before."

"Yes, I assumed that, but you don't kill anymore, right?"

"No, I don't and I haven't for many years, but I did before."

"I don't care, it doesn't matter, I know what you are and I know who you are."

"Ariel, would you like a glass of mineral water?"

"Sure, thanks."

I stepped over to the stove and removed the lid from the skillet and stirred the food and then put the lid back on it and then I took a bottle of mineral water from the counter. I opened the bottle and poured the water into a crystal glass and handed it to Ariel. "Here you go, Ariel, would it upset you if I drank a glass of blood?"

"No, I don't mind."

"Thanks, I opened the refrigerator and took out the pitcher of blood and poured some blood into one of the crystal glasses and sat down at the table next to Ariel. I looked at Ariel while I drank from my glass.

"It doesn't bother me Alexander."

"Thanks." Just then – Antoinette walked into the room.

Ariel sat her glass of water down on the table. "Oh, Antoinette you look like you are dressed for battle."

"Yes, sister, the black denim jeans, black boots and black turtleneck are a bit much, not to mention the hip holster, don't you think?"

"Not really Alexander, you know how I love to dress for the occasion." I guessed from the look on Ariel's face that Alexander had failed – to fill Ariel in on tonight's events.

Ariel glanced over at Alexander and then looked back at me. "Aren't you just meeting with the kids tonight?"

I waited for Alexander to explain tonight's events to Ariel. I watched him turn his head toward her.

"Well, Ariel, yes we are meeting with the kids and we are hoping to get them away from Luke, without a fight."

Ariel looked confused. "Is there going to be fighting, is this dangerous?"

"There could be a fight if Luke resists, I am sorry I didn't want to worry you."

"Really, Alexander it is ok for you to tell me what's going on, I'd rather know what's happening than be kept in the dark about everything."

"I am sorry."

"It's ok, so Antoinette what's in your hip holster?"

"Syringes full of vampire anesthesia."

"What is vampire anesthesia?"

"It is Alexander's own concoction for vampires because vampires don't sleep, but one stick in the neck with this stuff and they will be out in a matter of seconds, it goes straight to their brain."

I watched while Ariel turned to Alexander. "Alexander, is there anything I can do to help?"

"Yes Ariel, I would like you to spend the night with us and wait here until we get back. I will set the alarm and while we are gone please do not open the door for anyone."

"How long will you be gone?"

"Not too long maybe only a half hour."

"Ok tomorrow is Saturday and we don't have to work but I don't have any of my clothes with me."

I laughed. "That's not a problem Ariel, Antoinette has a collection of clothes big enough to clothe an entire city."

"Funny, brother, I think your dinner is burning."

I got up and took the skillet off the stove and fixed Ariel's plate and set it on the table. "Here you go, one gourmet Greek dinner!"

"Thank you Alexander, it looks great."

"Now, I will leave you with Antoinette while I go to my room and change my clothes."

"Ok, I am starving."

Alexander left and I looked over at Ariel. "Ariel I am going to run upstairs and sort through some clothes for you, I have some brand new clothes that have never been worn. When you are done eating why don't you just come up to the second floor."

"Ok, thanks Antoinette."

I left the kitchen and went to my room, I loved the double vaulted ceilings and huge stone fireplace. I looked at my four poster bed with chiffon drapes that hung on all four poles of the bed and even though I didn't sleep I still lay on my bed and often read. My antique oak wardrobe held extra clothing that didn't fit into my closet. I opened it up and began sorting through clothes. I started a pile of clothing on the bed that I thought Ariel could use, I didn't know how long she might be with us. I heard Ariel's voice in the hallway.

"Antoinette, where are you?"

I popped my head out of my bedroom door, "In here."

Ariel walked into my room. "Oh, this is awesome, I just love it."

"Thank you, I do love decorating. Here Ariel you can take these things, they are brand new. There are a couple of designer sweat suits and a night gown, robe, some slippers and a few blouses and some jeans, although you will have to roll the legs of the jeans up a bit."

"Thanks, that's more than I will probably need I plan on going home tomorrow."

I just looked at her and smiled. It was obvious that she didn't grasp the severity of her situation. If we took Mia, Tara and Dorian away from Luke, he would even be more furious and Ariel's life would never be the same again. My guess was that she was going to be with us for a while. "Well, whatever Ariel, if you need anything else, just let me know."

Ariel picked up the pile of clothing and held it in her arms. "Will I be bunking with you tonight Antoinette?"

I smiled and was glad that Ariel couldn't hear my thoughts. "Are you totally nuts woman?"

"No, Ariel, I will put you in a room next to Alexander's on the main floor. I think that he will feel better if you are closer to him."

"Alright, thanks."

Ariel followed me downstairs and – into the guest room that was next to Alexander's room. We walked in. "Ariel, you will find this very comfortable, there is a gas fireplace and the remote is sitting on the mantel, just turn it on whenever you need it. Alexander and I don't ever get cold and I light my fireplace just for decoration. The bedding is brand new and there is a small bathroom through that door."

"This room is awesome, the antique bed and dresser are beautiful, did you decorate this room too Antoinette?"

"Yes, I decorated the entire house."

"Oh, you missed your calling you should have been an interior decorator."

"Thank you Ariel, but I am not really that gifted, I've just had a lot of years to practice."

Ariel laughed. "I think I will just take a quick shower and maybe put on the sweats and slippers."

"That's great, I think Alexander is about ready to leave, we will see you when we get back, please remember what Alexander said about not answering the door while we are gone."

I walked out of Ariel's room and found Alexander standing in the foyer.

"Antoinette, is she all settled in?"

"Yes – I gave her some clothes and she is in the shower."

"Thanks sis, I really appreciate it. The alarm is set and I grabbed two more syringes with anesthesia, just in case."

"Ok, let's go", I said and pulled the door closed and we left the house.

* * *

Alexander and Antoinette had left and I was alone in this huge house. All of a sudden I found myself wondering if Alexander were right, "What if Luke really did want to change me, or even worse, kill me?" Both Alexander and Antoinette seemed really worried. I grabbed the remote from the fireplace and turned it to a low flame setting and then stepped into the bathroom to shower. After my shower I dressed in the designer sweat suit and put on the oversized pair of slippers, they would do for the evening. I walked over the huge queen sized antique oak bed and lay down on it. "Everything around me seemed so surreal. I was in love with a vampire, a real vampire that I had only known for a month and I was in hiding from another vampire that wanted to kill me. Things like this don't happen in the real world!" That's what I kept telling myself, but this is real, as real as I am lying on this bed. I closed my eyes and thought for a moment, "A month ago I was blissfully unaware that vampires existed. What else existed that I don't know about? What did my future hold? I wondered. The only thing that I did know for sure was that I was hopelessly in love with Alexander and wanted to be with him forever!"

11

THE RESCUE

Antoinette and I left the house and we arrived at the school just a few minuets before ten o'clock. We stood at the corner of a building just across from the maintenance building. We had a good view of the main doors. I wasn't sure what to expect, "Were the kids prepared to leave Luke now, if they could? Were we walking into a trap?" I wondered. "Antoinette, it is almost ten o'clock, I hope they show up."

"They will, I know it. You know I just realized that we really don't have a plan."

"What do you mean?"

"Well, if the kids are prepared to leave and if we have to fight I think we need to discuss that for a moment?"

"Ok, sister it's simple, if anything goes wrong, you run with the kids and I'll stay here."

"No, I am not leaving you, but I have another idea that might help. I think that we should be closer to them. We could get on the roof just over the doors."

"Good, idea lets go."

We quickly moved toward the maintenance building and in one quick swoop jumped to the roof and positioned ourselves over the front doors. "This is a good spot Alexander if we need to we can drop down from the roof and be right next to the kids. Now, back to our discussion, if we need to run with them I think that you should be the one to run and I stay. I can catch up to you I am a lot faster than you."

"Antoinette, I am not leaving you with four vampires, forget it."

"It's not about you or me anymore, you know that. We have talked about this before our work is going to continue to put us in dangerous situations."

"Well, I am sorry, I am not leaving you so it's my way or no way, I stay."

I looked at Alexander and knew that there was no point in arguing with him, but I also knew that I wasn't going to leave him either. It was past ten and I was starting to worry. "Had Luke discovered their plan and disposed of them?" All of a sudden I saw the doors of the maintenance building open and Dorian walked out, he was alone. He stood still for a moment and then the doors – opened again and Tara walked out. The door opened once more and Mia walked out and stood next to them.

I heard Tara's voice. "Mia, are they here?"

"I can't tell Tara."

I could sense their fear. "Mia we are above you, on the roof."

"Oh, Antoinette you came, thanks, can you help us get away from Luke?"

That was all we needed to hear. Alexander and I jumped from the roof and landed directly in front of the kids. "Yes, that's why we are here, but we have to go now."

All of a sudden the doors of the maintenance building flew open and Luke, Matt, Jason and Darla leapt out. They were ready to fight. In one quick motion I pushed Dorian, Mia and Tara behind me, but to my surprise Mia stepped back out from behind me and stood along side me. She glanced at me briefly and I saw the fear in her eyes as she prepared herself to fight.

Alexander stood on my other side. So it was the three of us against four of them, I sensed that Tara and Dorian were scared. I turned to them "When I tell you to run, you run and wait for us on the other side of the building, ok."

"Ok", Tara said.

Luke looked as cocky as ever. "I've been waiting for this opportunity Alexander ever since I first saw you."

"Same here Luke."

I whispered to Dorian and Tara and told them to back up.

All of a sudden Luke jumped at Alexander, they collided with such force that even as a vampire it was impossible for me to see what was happening.

Matt and Jason lunged at me and I tossed Matt aside momentarily to fight with Jason. After pushing Jason away I was able to get one of my injectors out and when Matt leapt back at me, I stuck him in the neck and in two seconds he went down. I don't think the other vampires realized what had happened to him. Alexander was still fighting with Luke. I looked out of the corner of my eye at Mia she was doing her best with Darla but she was no match for Darla's fighting expertise.

I saw Antoinette out of the corner of my eye standing next to Matt and then all of a sudden Matt went down and didn't move. Just then Darla lunged at me again and I stepped to the side to avoid her.

"Come here Mia."

She jumped at me again and then I felt her on me, she was squeezing my neck and I felt a tremendous amount of pressure in my head.

"Hold still Mia, so I can rip your head off."

I didn't know what to do. I was still staring at Matt, lying motionless on the ground. He looked like he was sleeping. I just wanted Darla to be like Matt, unconscious and then all of a sudden I felt her release her grip on my neck and I watched while she slumped slowly the ground like Matt. Antoinette looked over at me.

I looked over at Mia. "Good job Mia." Jason lunged at me again and pushed me sideways, I hit the wall of the building. All of a sudden, from out of nowhere I saw them, Zack and Jeremy. They moved so fast and stopped near us. Zack grabbed Luke away from Alexander and threw him hard, he hit the building and rolled and then stood up. Jeremy yanked Jason off me and tossed him aside. Luke knew what he was up against and called his friends to a retreat and they quickly disappeared. They left Matt and Darla lying on the cement, unconscious. Zack and Jeremy looked over at Matt and Darla and then back at me.

"They are sleeping I'll explain it to you later." I looked over and saw Darla lying on the ground motionless next to Matt and assumed that Alexander had given Mia one of his injectors with anesthesia to use on Darla.

We all stood there momentarily. I looked over at Mia. "Good job."

"Thanks."

Then I looked at Tara and Dorian. "Are you two ok?"

"Yes, Antoinette."

I looked over at Zack. "How did you find me again?"

Zack just smiled.

I turned to Alexander. "Alexander, I would like you to meet Zack and Jeremy."

Alexander stepped toward them. "Thank you both for your help tonight and for saving Antoinette the other night at the dance."

Jeremy looked at Alexander. "No problem dude glad to help."

Alexander stepped away from everyone. "We had better get out of here and get back to the house, Ariel is there alone."

I turned to Mia, Dorian and Tara. "We are going to take you guys back to our house you will be safe there."

Mia smiled. "Yes, thanks."

I looked over at Alexander and read his thoughts he had been thinking the same thing that I had. I turned back to Zack and Jeremy. "Would you two like to come back to the house with us? We could use the extra protection on the way home."

Zack stepped away from Jeremy and took a step toward me. "Sure Antoinette, anything to help you just lead the way!"

12

THE CHANGE AND OFF TO ALASKA

We arrived at the house and stood on the front porch. I unlocked the door and stepped inside and then entered the security code on the alarm pad. Everyone followed me inside and I turned around to face them. "Alright, please follow Antoinette and I into the living room and have a seat, you are safe here." Just as we entered the living room Ariel walked in.

"Oh, Alexander you are back."

I stepped toward her and hugged her.

"Yes, Ariel everything went as planned." I looked over at Mia, Tara and Dorian who sat huddled together on the couch and I saw them staring at Ariel, then I noticed Zack and Jeremy staring at her also. I wondered if Ariel would be safe around them.

I knew that my brother was worried about the other vampires being around Ariel. I tried – to read Zack's thoughts, but I couldn't. I read Jeremy's instead and knew that they meant her no harm. I already knew that Mia and Tara and Dorian also meant her no harm. I looked over at Alexander. "It's ok Alexander, she is safe."

Jeremy looked over at Alexander. "No worries dude, we spend most of our time patrolling the clubs and college campuses helping humans in trouble."

"Alexander smiled. "Thanks, guys."

I turned to Mia, Dorian and Tara and by the way that they looked I knew that they were probably very hungry. "Are you three hungry?"

Mia answered me. "Yes, Antoinette."

"Are you all ok around Ariel?"

"Yes Antoinette, we really don't want to hurt anyone, we've been surviving on leftovers from Luke and the others we haven't killed yet."

"Well, that would explain why all of you look undernourished. Would you like some blood? I mean a cup of blood?"

Mia looked at Tara and Dorian and then back at me. "Yes, thanks."

Zack looked over at me. "Antoinette – can I help you?"

"Sure Zack thanks." I don't know why I had told him yes, I really didn't need help but I had answered instinctively. Zack followed me into the kitchen. "Would you please grab that tray from the counter and put it on the table for me?" I asked him and then walked to the refrigerator and opened it up. I took out the pitcher of blood and set it on the tray that sat on the table and then I went to the cabinet and took out seven cups and sat them on the tray. I assumed everyone except Ariel of course, would have a cup of blood. I grabbed the bottle of mineral water that Alexander had opened earlier and a crystal glass for Ariel and sat them both on the tray.

Zack was smiling. "Antoinette, your house is really very lovely, just like you."

I smiled back, "Thanks Zack, we just bought it about four months ago, and this is our second semester teaching at the school. What do you and Jeremy do other than save women in distress?" I said and smiled.

Zack smiled back at me. "We stay busy during the day roaming around the city, looking for crimes in progress and then at night we hang out at clubs in the downtown area looking for people to help."

I laughed. Zack had an awesome personality. "That's right I forgot you are Billy the Kid and Jesse James."

"About that Antoinette, I owe you an apology?"

"I can't image for what, you've like saved my vampire life, like twice now."

Zack tilted his head down. "Yes but I wasn't really truthful with you, I mean about being Billy the Kid and Jesse James, we aren't really them - but we did know them and we rode with them years ago. That was after we were changed, but you know how that goes, it's never the same after."

I smiled, "That's ok, Zack, no worries. I figured that you weren't really them. So tell me, how did you know where to find me, twice now? I am guessing that you are gifted like I am."

"Yes, I can see things and sense things, like just a little while ago in the living room when you tried to read my thoughts."

"Yes, but I couldn't."

"That's because I blocked you out."

"You can do that?"

"Yes."

"I've never heard of that gift before, blocking someone from reading your thoughts."

"Well, I've got it."

I smiled. "Zack, would you please carry the tray into the living room for me?"

Zack picked up the tray and I followed him into the living room.

"Please just set it down on the coffee table."

I looked over at Mia, Tara and Dorian, "Ok, you three drink up, as much as you want, there is plenty more where that came from." I watched while they poured a cup of blood and gulped it down quickly. I knew that they were extremely hungry and I didn't want any accidental mishaps around Ariel.

Mia set her cup down. "So, what will happen to us now, Antoinette?"

"Well, Mia, that is up to you." I looked over at Alexander and he stepped away from Ariel and walked toward us and then sat down in a chair that faced the couch. Alexander looked over at the kids. "Why don't you tell me a little about yourselves and what your lives have been like?"

Mia cleared her throat. "Well, Alexander my parents died in a plane crash last year and I went into foster care, that's where I met Tara and then we ran away and were living on the streets for a while. Two vampires found us and changed us and then about a week later we met Luke and the others and we have been with them ever since, Dorian just joined us about a month ago."

"Ok, Mia thanks." I looked over at Dorian and he sat his cup down and smiled.

"I ran away from a bad home and bad parents and was living on the street. Luke changed me about a month ago and I haven't killed on my own either."

Next I looked over at Tara she had hardly said a word the entire night.

"Well, like Mia said we met in foster care, but I have been in foster care for a long time, both my parents are in prison with life sentences and believe me they belong there."

I looked over at my brother. I knew that Alexander wanted to talk to them about changing back to humans and he was concerned about Zack and Jeremy hearing about our work. Intuitively I knew that Zack and Jeremy would not say a word to anyone and that our secret would be safe with them. I nodded at Alexander.

"Antoinette, would you please re-fill the pitcher of blood?"

"Sure Alexander."

After Antoinette picked up the tray from the coffee table and left the room I turned to Mia, Tara and Dorian. What would you three say if I told you that I could make you human again?" They looked confused. "I am serious Antoinette and I are doctors and we can definitely change you back to a human that is, if you want to be human again."

Mia was the first to speak. "Alexander, how is this possible?"

Antoinette had returned with the tray and sat it on the coffee table.

"Antoinette, I just asked them if they would like to be changed back to humans."

Mia spoke again. "Antoinette, is it possible?"

"Yes, Mia, this is the work that Alexander and I do. We have been doing this in England and Europe for a while now and have changed a lot of vampires back to being human. We definitely can make you human again?"

Zack and Jeremy looked shocked. I stepped over to Zack and stood next to him. "Yes, Zack we have developed a procedure to change vampires back to humans that is what we are doing here, trying to help vampires who can't cope anymore and don't want to be vampires."

Zack smiled at me. "Well, Antoinette, we share a similar purpose Jeremy and I realized years ago that we had to find some good in what happened to us and we've been protecting the innocent since then. We only feed on killer's like you do."

Mia leaned up from the couch. "Alexander, I still don't understand how this is possible."

"Mia, it is a four hour surgical procedure. I will repair some damaged genes, your vein system and your organs. There is absolutely no risk, especially with younger vampires like you guys, it is perfectly safe. Let me explain the process to you a little more in detail and then you three can discuss it."

Mia spoke again. "But, what would happen to us afterwards, I mean how long does it take to recover from the surgery?"

Tara spoke next. "I don't care I want to do it, my answer is yes."

"Me too", Dorian said.

"Let me answer all your questions first and then you can decide. You would be anesthetized and unconscious during the surgery." Mia interrupted me.

"Is that what happened to Matt?"

"Yes Mia, I have developed an anesthesia that works on vampires. I won't go into detail about the surgery, it is a very complicated procedure but after you are unconscious I repair some damaged genes and then introduce by catheter, a very – very – slow – drip blood transfusion – it's not really a transfusion per say, as vampires do not have blood in their veins. I am putting blood back into the veins slowly while the veins repair their selves. The procedure takes less time to work on younger vampires because there is not as much damage to their body tissues, veins and organs compared to the older vampires that are over three hundred years old. Once the veins are functioning and blood is reproducing itself, the extra muscle tissue and extra bone starts reducing and the lymphatic system starts shrinking back to a normal size. Then I look at each organ one by one and if they are not responding I induce an electrical shock – by surgical probe to stimulate and awaken them – and then the human body takes over from there. The calcification process, the hardening of the bones and teeth start to soften and return to normal calcification in about a week."

Tara spoke. "It sounds amazing I mean I've wanted my life back since this first happened to me. But what about afterwards, where would we go? I don't ever want to be out on the street again."

Dorian turned his head to Tara. "I don't even care about that Tara, anything is better than this."

I interrupted them. "You will not be out on the street, we have money and the means to help you guys get set up and start new lives. We have some very dear friends in Alaska, Charles and Eloise. They were vampires and now they are humans. Their kids are grown and they have offered to take you three in and want to be your foster family. They are wonderful people and you would be really safe with them."

"Yes, I want to do it", Tara said.

"Me, too", Dorian said.

Mia turned to Antoinette. "Antoinette, is there any danger during the surgery?"

"Absolutely not, Mia, it is perfectly safe, I promise."

"That's good enough for me. Ok Antoinette Tara and Dorian will go first and I will go last."

Mia looked at me and for a split second I read her thoughts. She had no intention of changing back to a human.

Zack and Jeremy had been extremely quiet during the conversation. I looked over at Zack. "You guys ok, with all of this?"

Zack stepped toward me. "Absolutely Antoinette, what can we do to help?"

"Thanks guys. Alexander and I will both need to perform the surgery, and Ariel can keep an eye on things inside the house. Could you and Jeremy stand guard outside the house and make sure that we have no unexpected company."

"You got it, Antoinette."

I watched while Zack and Jeremy left the room and walked outside.

I turned to the kids. "Ok let's go upstairs to the clinic and get started, we need to do this right away so that we can get you guys out of here as soon as possible." Alexander led the way upstairs to the clinic and Mia, Tara and Dorian, Ariel and I followed. Alexander turned to face the kids.

"Ok, who wants to go first?"

Tara responded. "I will."

"Ok, Tara you come with Antoinette and I. Ariel can sit with Mia and Dorian in the waiting room.

Antoinette and I entered the operating room suite and Tara changed into a hospital gown and got up on the table.

"Ok, Tara, I am going to place the anesthesia mask over your face, ok?"

"Ok, Antoinette."

We began the surgery.

* * *

Eight hours later, both Tara and Dorian were in the recovery room and Alexander and I walked out into the waiting room to talk with Mia. I already knew that Mia had decided that she was not going to have the procedure performed but I didn't know why. "Ok, Mia, have you changed your mind yet?"

"I am sorry Antoinette I don't want to change back. I only said that so that Tara and Dorian would do it, I knew that they wouldn't unless I agreed."

"Yes, I had suspected that much, but I would like to know why?"

"Well, I am still angry at Luke and the others and I was thinking about you and Alexander and how you are trying to help vampires. I thought that I could help too."

"Well, Mia that is very admirable but what about school? I mean you are only sixteen years old?"

"I am going back to Lincoln High and I am going to graduate, I am not afraid, I mean after all I am a vampire, so I shouldn't be afraid of a few vampires and I apparently have some kind of gift. Maybe you could teach me how to fight?"

I looked over at Mia. "What do you mean gift?"

"Well, like when I was fighting Darla and I put her to sleep."

I looked at my brother and then back at Mia. "Didn't Alexander give you one of his injector's to use?"

Alexander looked back over at me. "No, Antoinette I didn't, I assumed that you had given her one of your injectors when I saw Darla lying next to Matt."

"No I didn't Alexander." I looked back at Mia. "Mia, tell me what happened."

"I am not sure, when I was fighting Darla she had grabbed hold of my neck and was squeezing it and my head was hurting badly then I saw you fighting with Matt and he went down and was unconscious. All I could think about was that I wanted Darla off me and sleeping like Matt and then all of a sudden she just let go and collapsed to the ground."

Alexander and I exchanged glances. It was obvious that Mia did have a gift. Not too many vampires had gifts. I smiled and then looked at Alexander again. The look on my brother's face had told me that it was my decision to accept Mia's help with our work. "Mia, I think you are a very tough young lady and I think that we could definitely use your help. You can stay here with us while you go to school."

"Oh, thank you Antoinette and thank you Alexander."

"Mia, have you thought about what you might want to do later, I mean after you graduate?"

"Yes, Antoinette, I always wanted to be a doctor."

I smiled. "Good choice, let's go in and visit with Tara and Dorian, they should be awake now."

"Antoinette, while you and Mia go see the kids I am going to call Charles and see if he can come down and pick the kids up day after tomorrow. We need to get them out of here as soon as possible."

"Ok, Alexander." I led Mia into the recovery room. Both Tara and Dorian were in the same room. They were both awake now but still a little groggy. I walked to Tara's bedside.

"Hello Tara, how are you feeling?"

"Strange and tired, did everything go ok, am I human now?"

"Yes, Tara everything went fine and indeed you are human. You will be very tired until your blood starts replenishing itself. Mia is here."

Mia stepped next to the bed. "Tara I am here and I will be checking on you all night, ok. You just get some rest."

"Ok, Mia, are you going next?"

I interrupted them before Mia could answer Tara. I knew that Mia did not want to upset Tara by telling her that she was not going to change back. "Tara you need to rest, we are going to talk to Dorian for a moment, ok?"

"Ok, Antoinette."

Mia followed me over to Dorian's bedside. "Hello Dorian, how are you feeling?"

"Tired, like Tara, am I human too?"

"Yes, Dorian, everything went fine."

"Thank you Antoinette, thank you so much."

"Your welcome, you get some rest now and Mia is here also."

"Dorian I will check on you guys all night, get some rest."

"Ok, Mia."

Mia and I stepped outside of the recovery room and into the hallway.

"Antoinette, I just can't believe it they are human, they are really human?"

"Yes, Mia, the procedure works." I led Mia back to the waiting room area. Alexander had returned and was sitting with Ariel. Ariel looked up at me.

"Hello Antoinette, Alexander told me that the kids are doing just fine. I am so proud of both of you for helping them. Alexander is a genius."

I looked at Alexander's face and despite the fact that he was a vampire and somewhat emotionless, like most vampires, his face just glowed with pride at Ariel's comment.

I smiled. "Yes, Ariel, Alexander is a genius" I said. I looked over at Mia. "Ok, Mia why don't you come with me and I will show you to your room." Mia followed me down the staircase to the second floor. "I have the entire second floor, it is ten rooms and I can't possibly use all of them." I walked to the end of the hallway and stopped and then opened the door we walked in. "This room is big and has a fireplace and a bathroom."

"It's beautiful Antoinette."

"There isn't much furniture in here right now, but tomorrow we will go shopping and you can pick some things out, also I will give you a credit card for personal use."

"Antoinette I don't know how to thank you."

"No thanks are necessary I respect your decision to not want to change back and help us with our work. I had better check on Zack and Jeremy, they are still outside."

I left Mia in her room and walked downstairs and out the front door, it was just getting light out. "Zack, Jeremy, are you guys still out here?"

They both dropped down from the rooftop.

"Here we are Antoinette."

"Hey guys, careful with the jumping from the roof thing in daylight. Our next door neighbor, Mrs. Crabitz is really nosey and is probably armed with binoculars."

They laughed. "Sure, thing Antoinette."

"Hey guys, thanks for keeping watch, the kids are out of surgery and doing fine."

"That's great Antoinette, Jeremy and I had been talking about the procedure and we are still pretty amazed at the fact that you can do this."

"Thanks Zack, we are hopeful to help a lot of vampires now and in the future."

"So, what are your plans for the future Antoinette?"

Zack's question took me by surprise. "Well, someday Alexander and I hope to give our practice over to other vampire doctors and then live our lives as humans, I mean marry, and have children and grow old, you know."

"That sounds great Antoinette, like something I would want to do later also."

"Well, you guys just let us know when you are ready and we will help you change back too. Zack where do you and Jeremy live, is Portland your home?"

"No, we were just passing through on our way to Alaska, when we bumped into you and then we decided to stay for a while?"

"Where are you guys living, though?"

"You know, just here and there."

It was obvious to me that they didn't have a home and I had an idea. The house that Charles and Eloise had given us was vacant and I thought the least I could do is offer to let them stay there, after all they had saved my life. "Hey guys, I have an idea we have another house, a few miles from here. It's vacant right now and we need someone to watch over it. It is bigger than this house and we have been planning to use it sort of as a hotel for patients. How would you like to stay there and take care of it for us?"

Zack and Jeremy looked at each other and then Zack turned his head back to me. "Sure, Antoinette, that would be great, it would be nice to have a place to hang out at."

"Great, you guys, I am going to run in and tell Alexander and then I am going to run you guys over to the house."

I watched while Antoinette walked away and I turned to Zack. "Dude, what are you doing, I thought we were heading up to Alaska?"

"I know Jeremy, but I still have that feeling that Antoinette is in danger."

"I thought that had passed, with what happened the other night in the gym."

"No, Jeremy, that wasn't it, it's something else. She is still in danger!

13

DANGER! CALICIA CLAIG'S COVEN

I sat in my medical clinic on the third floor in the house and had gone over the situation in my mind for the umpteenth time. The chess game had begun and it was Luke's move. Antoinette and I were on guard both at the school and at our house. The score was even and Luke couldn't stand it. We had taken Mia, Tara and Dorian from him and there was nothing he could do about it. Tara and Dorian were safe in Alaska with Charles and Eloise. Mia was staying with us and Zack and Jeremy were staying at the house that Charles and Eloise had donated to the clinic. I was growing more concerned about Ariel's safety and despite my attempts to make her understand the severity of the situation I knew that she did not understand the risks of dating a vampire. Antoinette entered the room and interrupted my thoughts.

"Alexander, I just had another vision, they are getting stronger."

I turned slightly in my chair and looked at my sister. "What did you see this time?"

"The visions are clearer now, I saw Ariel standing in a room, surrounded by Luke and the others."

"I don't know what else I can do Antoinette she won't listen to me she is talking about going back to her apartment. She doesn't seem to understand that she is in danger."

"You have to convince her, where is she now?"

"She's down in her room resting she wants to go back to her apartment tomorrow."

Alexander looked upset. "Well, why don't you go down and try and talk to her again, have you told her about my visions?"

"Yes, I was heading down to see her in just a few minutes anyway."

Antoinette and I walked out of my office and down to the second floor and Antoinette went to her room. I walked to the first floor and then down the hall and stopped in front of Ariel's door. I knocked, "Ariel, it's me."

"Come in Alexander." I sat up in my bed just as Alexander walked through the door. "Hi, what's up?"

I walked over and sat down on the edge of the bed next to her and smiled at her. Her red curly hair had been piled up on the top of her head and was held in place with a big clip. "You look really pretty."

"Thanks, Alexander?"

Ariel slid her body backwards on the bed and then leaned against the headboard.

"Scoot over", I said and moved my body beside her and then I put my arm around her. "Are you tired Ariel?"

"A little, it's almost midnight."

"Ariel, Antoinette has been having more visions about you."

"What kind of visions?"

"That you are in danger, she saw Luke and his friends standing around you in a room somewhere."

"Oh, Alexander it's been over a week now and you know how I feel about all of this. Luke has been a perfect student in my class all week and hasn't smarted off to me once. I really don't think that he intends to harm me."

"Trust me Ariel, it's an act, Luke is just buying time until he can get you alone."

"I don't think so Alexander, I just don't see it that way." I rested my head on Alexander's shoulder. "I know you are worried about me, and I love you for that, but it's ok."

"Ariel, I know Luke and how he thinks."

"Well Alexander, I can't stay here forever, I mean I do have a life and there are things that I need at my apartment."

"Ariel I will take you back to your apartment to collect whatever you need but please just stay here a while longer with us. I am really worried about you I couldn't bear it if anything happened to you."

"I am sure that I would be safe at home."

"No you won't be and if you decide to go back to your apartment, Antoinette and I will have to stand guard outside of it all night long!"

"You would do that, wouldn't you?"

"Yes, I would Ariel."

"Oh, Alexander I can't wait until this is over."

I knew that Ariel was still not grasping the reality of her situation. She was dating a vampire now and her life would never be the same, she would always be in danger because of me."

"Ariel, it will never be over."

"What do you mean Alexander?"

"Well the more vampires that Antoinette and I help the more attention we will draw to ourselves and there will always be danger, for us and for anyone associated with us."

"I don't understand?"

"As long as you are with me, you will always be in danger. Maybe we shouldn't be together. If it weren't for me, Luke wouldn't be after you now, maybe you would be safer if you had nothing to do with me?" I wished I hadn't said it, but it was too late. The look on her face told me that I had upset her terribly.

Ariel sat up in bed and turned her head toward me. "Alexander don't you say that - you can't be serious? Why would you say such a thing to me?"

"Calm down Ariel, I am sorry. I didn't mean it."

"Ok, but don't say anything like that to me ever again. We belong together."

I knew that she was right, we did belong together. I turned my body toward her and wrapped my arms around her and pulled her close. "Ariel can I ask you a personal question?"

"Of course you can Alexander."

"Are you a virgin?"

"Absolutely, twelve years of catholic school before college and my parents were very strict, but I am grateful to them for that. I don't believe in pre-marital relations."

"Neither do I."

I looked at Alexander. "What was it like back then Alexander, I mean in the eleventh-century between a woman and a man."

I smiled. "It was very simple and innocent back then. The excitement was just dating and getting to know someone. People dated for months before they even kissed, families were involved in the dating process and people were engaged for at least a year or longer before they got married."

"Are you serious? It's definitely a lot different now."

"Yes, it is, things have changed, but it doesn't have to be like that. It's sad that more young people don't understand the importance of waiting to be intimate until they are married."

"I agree, but a lot of young women don't understand that if a guy pressure's you to be intimate, he only wants one thing." I nestled my head against Alexander's chest and then briefly looked up at his face and I knew that I was absolutely loved and safe wrapped in his arms.

* * *

"Why Luke, I haven't heard from you in ages, where are you calling from?"

"Never mind where I am Calicia, we will get to that later."

"I had suspected that another vampire would have disposed of you by now Luke. I never thought that you would make it out on your own away from the safe haven of your home and coven here in Canada."

"I am not the little boy that you remember Calicia."

"Don't you mean Mother?"

"No Calicia, you're not my mother, you're my step mother."

"Yes, I am your step-mother and your only family since your father's untimely death."

"It was timely enough for you to take over my father's coven and you wasted no time in doing so. He fell for your beauty and charm, that tall body and blonde hair and blue eyes and those blood red lips and fingernails, it was his undoing, but it won't be mine."

"Why, Luke it was all too easy – once he was gone, who were the others going to follow, you or an experienced three-hundred year old leader, like me. So boy, what is it that you want of me after all this time?"

"I have some news that I thought you might be interested in, but it will cost you."

"Cost me how?"

"I want money, Calicia, big money. I have started a coven of my own and it will bear my father's name."

"I seriously doubt that you have anything that I would be interested in Luke, but I'll humor you, what is it?"

"Ok Calicia, what would you say if I told you that I just had a run in with two vampires and fought them and they put two of my vampires to sleep."

"What do you mean Luke, vampires can't sleep?"

"Well two of my vampires did sleep for over an hour they were – completely unconscious and then awoke. They seem unharmed and it just so happens that the two vampires we fought are also doctors, they are from England."

Calcia, cleared her throat. "You say they are from England, Luke?"

"Yes, why have you heard of them?"

"I believe, so, if they are the same vampires that I have heard about, some covens are looking for them, tell me more about them, two brothers right?"

"Good try Calicia, but no, it's a brother and sister."

"Well, Luke you surprise me you passed my little test. Yes, then I am very interested in them and their medicines that make vampires sleep. Can you bring them to me, dear boy? Why don't you come home to Canada it just hasn't been the same since you left."

"Yes, I know what you mean, you must miss ordering me around and no I cannot bring them to you. One stick of that injector and I would be out before I hit the ground, but I can bring you something better than the both of them, for now and the price is high."

"What can you bring me Luke?"

"The male vampire's human mate, he would do anything to save her."

"Dear boy, I do believe I've misjudged you, perhaps money should not be your only reward. I have grown tired these last few years of ruling alone, perhaps you might reconsider and come home after all and sit at my side!"

"Calicia, for a split second you almost had me, but I know you all too well, the price is one-million dollars, a tiny fraction of what you have, one-million dollars for the girl."

"Ok, agreed Luke, when?"

"I'll let you know."

14

ARIEL IS ABDUCTED

Alexander had asked me not to leave the school without him or Antoinette but I couldn't help it. My class had ended early and I hadn't been home in over a week and I needed to get some clothes and personal items to take back to Alexander's house. I had decided to stay with him for a while, like he suggested. I had started to think that maybe Alexander had over reacted a little as to what Luke's intent had been with me – over a week had passed and Luke had sat in my class and been the perfect student. I decided to drive to my apartment and grab a few things as quickly as I could so I locked up my classroom, stopped by the office to check my mail-box and left the school. I drove to my apartment and parked my beetle in my parking space and then walked to my apartment and unlocked my door and stepped in. "Home, sweet home", I said and took in a breath of air and then closed the door. I hadn't realized how much I had missed my home. I glanced around at the small living room, dinning room and kitchen. I had spent a lot of extra money decorating my apartment and my landlord had allowed me to paint my living room walls blue, one of my favorite colors. I walked in my bedroom and opened up my closet and removed my suitcase and then sat it on my bed and opened it up. I walked over to my dresser and opened drawer after drawer and began picking through my clothes to choose what to take back to Alexander's house, next I walked to my closet and did the same thing and then I walked into my bathroom to grab some toiletry items. "That about does it", I thought to myself. All of a sudden I heard the creaking of a door, it sounded like the front door of my apartment. I thought that I had closed the door all the way, but maybe I hadn't and the wind blew it open. Despite that thought, I felt the little hairs on my arm stand up and I got goose bumps and felt a shiver, something was wrong. I heard another noise, a footstep then another. I stepped toward my closet and then stepped inside of it. There was no place else to hide. I stood inside the closet and held my breath. I heard more footsteps and then I knew that someone was in the bedroom. "Go, away, please just go away", I thought. Several thoughts rushed through my head and I wondered if it were the maintenance man they sometimes came into the apartments to inspect them or fix something when tenants weren't home. That thought gave me some comfort for just a minute and then I heard a voice. "Ariel, you may as well come out of the closet we know you are in there." It was Luke's voice. I remained still. "Come out or I will come in and get you." His voice had been condescending and playful, like when two children are playing, hide and seek. I stepped out from the closet and faced Luke, Darla, Matt and Jason. I looked directly at Luke, "What are you doing in here?" I tried to display some authority both as the tenant of the apartment and as his teacher, but I could tell by the look on his face it hadn't worked.

"So, little Ariel is all alone without big bad Alexander to save her?"

His comment startled me. "What did he mean save me", I'd thought. "Did he intend to kill me?" and then I knew that Alexander had been right. Luke had been waiting for the opportunity to catch me alone and I had played right into his hands. "I asked you what you are doing here and I expect an answer Luke."

"Brave little Ariel too, Calicia is going to love you."

I knew that I couldn't fight one vampire, let alone four but I had to try and all of a sudden I lunged forward and delivered a kick to Luke and connected with his jaw. It had absolutely no impact on him.

"Funny, Ariel, this would have been easier if you would just cooperate, but I see that is not going to happen."

All of a sudden I saw Luke's arm reaching toward me really fast and I felt a hard blow to the side of my head and then I saw blackness.

* * *

"Antoinette, where is she? She should be here by now, she knows to meet us after school in the parking lot and her car isn't here."

"Calm, down Alexander, she might have parked in the front of the school today, when we got here this morning the parking lot was full, remember. She is probably still in her classroom and got delayed or is talking with Principle Hines in his office."

"It has already been a half hour lets go and look for her."

I could see that Alexander was terribly upset and although I tried to comfort him I was just as worried, I had a nagging feeling deep down that something terrible had happened to Ariel. I followed Alexander to Ariel's classroom and watched while he tried the door.

"It's locked."

I watched while he knocked and then pounded on Ariel's classroom door.

"Ariel, Ariel are you in there? It's Alexander."

I turned to my brother. "Alexander, she's not here let's walk over to the office." I followed Alexander into the office and he greeted the secretary, Mrs. Teaple.

"Hello Mrs. Teaple, I was wondering if you have seen Ariel this afternoon, Antoinette and I were supposed to meet with her this evening."

"Oh yes, I saw Ariel a couple of hours ago, her class ended early today and she had mumbled something about running home to her apartment."

"Thank you Mrs. Teaple, have a good evening."

"You have a good evening too, Alexander."

I walked behind Alexander as he walked briskly out of the office and then back toward the parking lot to our Hummer.

"Antoinette, lets go to her apartment, can you drive I am going to try and call her cell phone."

I climbed into the Hummer and started it up and began driving while Alexander called Ariel on his cell phone and then I watched while he slammed his phone down on the seat. "It went straight to voice mail!" Alexander looked distraught and ran his hands through his hair. "Calm down, I am sure she is probably at her apartment right now and probably just left her cell phone in the car."

"I hope you are right Antoinette, if anything happens to her I will never forgive myself."

The minute I pulled the Hummer into the parking lot of Ariel's apartment we saw her little blue beetle parked in her spot. I looked over at Alexander. "See, I told you, she is still here."

We parked the Hummer and got out and I walked behind Alexander toward Ariel's apartment. When we reached her door we noticed that it was slightly ajar. Alexander called out to her, "Ariel."

There was no answer. Alexander pushed the apartment door open and rushed inside. I walked in behind him and we both just froze and gazed at the message scribbled on the living room wall. It appeared to be written in blood.

"Checkmate Alexander it's your move, I've got something you want and you will pay."

I turned my head toward Alexander. "Alexander, I am sorry, I am sure she is ok – the message says that he wants something from you."

"But you don't understand Antoinette, it is her blood on the wall, I can smell it - its Ariel's blood and there is so much blood."

I looked at the wall and knew that my brother was correct, it was an excessive amount of blood and there were two options to consider, either Ariel was dead or Luke had changed her.

Alexander looked over at me. "Antoinette, he's changed her!"

About the Author

The author, Shelly Stone started writing when she was a teenager and never really stopped. She lives with her dog Jake in South Dakota. She is part Chippewa Indian and has a great respect for nature. She writes a variety of books.

Visit with Shelly at themadwriter1.blog.com to see her other books or chat with her.

"Vampires 201", out in April 2014.
"Vampires 202, The Immortals", coming soon